Brews and Clues

A.N. Payton

Published by A.N. Payton, 2024.

Table of Contents

Chapter 1..1
Chapter 2..7
Chapter 3...15
Chapter 4...22
Chapter 5...34
Chapter 6...41
Chapter 7...50
Chapter 8...57
Chapter 9...69
Chapter 10..81
Chapter 11..88
Chapter 12..98
Chapter 13...103
Chapter 14...111
Chapter 15...124
Chapter 16...134
Chapter 17...140
Chapter 18...147
Chapter 19...154
Chapter 20...160
Chapter 21...164
Chapter 22...171
Chapter 23...177
Chapter 24...179
Want to Support the Author?..183
Acknowledgements...184
About the Author...185
Other Works by A.N. Payton...186

to everyone that pauses their true crime podcast to pick up their fantasy novel

Chapter 1

The wagon shook around me, somehow keeping the delicate glass jars and cups in place despite the harsh vibrations. Even the sign hanging below the window reading Brew-Tea-Ful, the name of my traveling potion wagon, remained perched on its hook. I ground my teeth around a tight smile and handed the customer her drink—a mild lavender healing tonic with the barest wisp of a smokey texture, perfect to ease a slight headache or mild pain that wouldn't go away—and pretended the shaking structure didn't bother me.

"Have a nice day," I said, the words sickly sweet, a pointed reminder to Brew that we had customers and it needed to behave. It rarely listened to me, but I could hope.

A young man stepped up to the window, coins in hand, and mouth open to place his order.

The wagon shook again.

"Just a moment." I ducked inside the narrow window before he could speak and lowered the wooden sash. The thin barrier shouldn't have been enough to block my words, but the customers wouldn't hear me if Brew didn't want them to.

I jabbed my finger toward the opposite wall. "You promised to behave today."

A fluff of ground herbs popped up from the jars along the back wall, sending the scent of cumin and basil into an earthy cloud through the air.

"Very mature." I waved my hand until the dust settled. "If you don't knock it off, I will turn this wagon around and take us home."

The floor creaked in discontentment, but the herbs didn't explode again—which I took as a good sign. I slowly turned back toward the customer window—sending a quick glance over my shoulder so Brew sensed my seriousness—and flipped the wooden sash back up, prepared to apologize to the young man outside.

Twin brown eyes, broody and intense, returned my stare less than a hand-span from my face. I yelped and jumped back, clutching at the rim of the inset basin to prevent a fall. The wagon shuttered again, quick and pulsed, a little laugh to say it had tried to warn me.

I put my hand over my pulsing heart as Leof, the town's investigative marshal, stuck his head inside. "I didn't mean to frighten you."

"No," I said. "Whatever you want, the answer is no." He opened his mouth, but I held my finger up the way I'd done to my wagon moments ago. "Don't try it. I'm not doing it."

He paused. "You don't even know what I want."

"I will not look at a dead body for you. I already told you; I am done."

Leof rolled his eyes. "One body disintegrates from an undiagnosed case of inferno-pox, and you're done working with me? Is that really all it takes to scare little ol' Rae?"

I pressed my lips together and looked down at the counter. It hadn't been the inferno-pox that worried me. The fact that a Disease Control and Research team from the capital investigated the situation riled me up. It reminded me I needed to prioritize caution over helping a friend, even Leof. If the king learned where I'd been hiding, I'd gladly choose the inferno-pox before returning to him.

"I won't do it, Leof. Find someone else." I reached for the sash.

Leof grabbed the other end and forced it back up. I strained, but didn't stand a chance against his werewolf strength. I dropped my hand.

"That was cute," he said. "Enough games. I have a dead guy and my people are saying suicide, but something feels off. You're the next best thing in this town."

I rolled my eyes. "You always know how to flatter a girl. But I can't, Leof. Not this time."

Leof tapped his fingers along the top of the serving counter. He bit his tongue, like he considered saying more. I hoped he didn't. I hoped he'd leave and stop scaring away my customers.

"He has the mark," Leof said, reluctantly.

I kept my face flat, but a sudden fist grabbed my chest.

"What mark?" I tried too hard to make my voice casual. It came out forced.

His eyes flicked to my wrist, where a careful concealment spell masked the outline of a simple dagger.

He looked back at me. The rich chocolate of wolf eyes met my gaze.

"You know the one."

Another Provider, here in Hallow's Promise? I bit my lip. It shouldn't have been possible.

Unless they were looking for me.

"Fine," I said. Leof's shoulders straightened, and he smirked. He knew he could convince me to go. "After this shift, I'll look at your body for ten minutes. Then I'm ignoring you for the rest of my life."

He winked. "Good luck with that."

****

The Central Campus for Mages and Magics ate up almost a quarter of Hallow's Promise. One side of the property boasted a beautiful rock-stacked structure with massive spiraling gray towers launching into the sky. A chorus of bells topped teach one, and they released a symphony of dings and dongs twice a day, at noon and midnight. It made me glad to live across town.

The west side of campus held a bowl-shaped pond where hungry koi snapped up the students' food-hall leftovers, and the bigger ones occasionally tried for a finger or two—though I hadn't seen it happen. In the springtime, the campus smelled like cherry blossoms and the color pink. But this time of year, as fall drew to a close and students studied for exit exams, it reminded me more of wet paper and desperation.

"And that's for you." I handed over a pomegranate tea, infused with a gentle happiness spell. Smooth steam slipped over the edge of the mug, releasing the slightest ginger notes. "Remember, drink it slowly, or the magic will be more intense, but for a shorter duration."

"Thank you." The student took her tea and let out a sigh of relief with the first sip as I watched her walk away. A warmth crawled up my chest and Brew's cupboard doors opened and closed a few times.

I patted the wagon's wall. "I know. Sometimes, it's all worth it." Leaving the capital to come to Hallow's Promise was the best decision I'd ever made.

Leof perched on a bench near the pond. He looked toward the fish, ripples swelling with their movements, but I knew he focused on me. If I tried to run, he'd come find me. The scene seemed to affect him.

I settled the closed sign outside the window and pulled down the sash. The wooden latch slid shut on its own, and the wagon hummed as it settled for the evening. I wiped down the counter, blew out the candles, and went through the door at the rear of the structure. A slight click told me Brew locked itself from the inside.

Leof stood as I approached. In another life, he would have been handsome and carefree, but the job had taken something precious from him long ago. Suspicion hugged the corners of his eyes. He saw the world in minute detail, but always waited for the worst to happen. He couldn't be much older than me—too young for such skepticism.

But I had my share of ghosts from the past, too.

I paused beside the wolf. We both watched the flashes of dancing koi. A heaviness rested in the silence. Someone had died, and we bore the responsibility of what must happen next.

"I'll give you ten minutes. Not a moment more," I said.

Leof nodded and didn't argue this time. We turned, heading toward the tether where Leof's steed, Cherry, shared a lead post with a handful of other mounts.

We passed Brew, and the marshal hesitated. "Do you need help moving that? We could put my horse on it."

I smiled and patted the wagon's side. "It'll get home later."

Leof frowned but didn't press me. He untied the lead, jumped into the saddle, and held out a hand for me. I didn't need help, but I clutched his palm anyway and let the Marshall pull me up. Cherry didn't flinch at her double load and flicked her ears curiously. I patted her side, and her scent of earth and hay comforted me.

Leof swung the reins and led us toward the dead man.

Chapter 2

A cluster of marshals and constables hugged a rugged single-story house at the edge of the Devote Alcove area of Hallow's Promise. The neighborhood consisted of mostly laborers, able to afford well-constructed homes, but not necessarily comfortable ones. Property lines allowed a bit of space for horse pastures or small plots. Hearty meal fires glowed through bone-paneled windows, and thick scents of stewed meat and roasted herbs made my stomach rumble.

Two men broke from the group and met us near the horse.

"We already told you we don't need the help, Marshal." One broad shoulder man stated, a red tint staining his face. He cast an angry glance at me, which I let fall away with a shrug. It wasn't the first time I'd received a less than a warm welcome, and it wouldn't be the last.

Leof shoved his shoulder into the man as we walked by. "Shut up, Castor. I outrank you."

I followed in the wolf's wake. Castor's anger turned hot behind me, flames trying to lick my back. A hint of my magic responded. It licked over the constable and settled down. It didn't perceive him as a threat.

The front door stood open. Several dusty impressions of shoe soles lined the floor in and out of the house. I rolled my eyes. The plethora of investigators trampling the scene would have worn away any small particles of evidence.

The house appeared modest. Simple, landscaped paintings hung along the walls. There was a quaint kitchen with a large wood stove, stone counters, and a rugged dining table in the center. Used candles perched in sconcesalong the walls, unlit despite the setting sun.

In the rear of the house, two more doors arched into darkness, but Leof didn't offer to show me those rooms. I didn't ask. The sooner I helped him and left, the better. I still had a few spells and syrups to brew for tomorrow's orders.

The dead man hung from the peaked rafters in the kitchen, beside the dining table. A frayed rope circled his neck with a slick knot on one side. His skin already held an orange hue and had red mottling at his bare feet where the blood had gathered with gravity. Heavy lids half covered vacant brown eyes. As Leof had mentioned, the simple outline of a dagger set into his skin paled beneath the ink without pulsing oxygenated blood.

Death cast an inhuman quality on the body. I knew the man had been alive days, maybe hours earlier, but now a heaviness clung to his form. He looked less real, less relatable.

Castor and the other constable followed behind us. I ignored his unhappy glowering and stepped closer to the body.

Castor made a noise.

"Shut up," Leof said. The other man's jaw clicked shut, but the rage didn't thin.

I ignored them, using the distraction to scan the room. A sterile edge covered the space. Everything felt too orderly, too well-placed. It made me want to put on a coat, even though winter hadn't touched the air yet.

"There's no blood," I said. The attention in the room shifted to me. I refused to hunch my shoulders or cower from the words I had to say. That part of me remained in the capital after I had fled.

"We didn't see any either," Leof replied.

I jerked my head toward the body swinging above us. "Know his name?"

Leof shook his head.

I turned to the table. The dead guy could have easily stood on the tabletop and secured the rope over the rafters. Even my rather short form could have done the same. Once he stepped off, the platform would be too far to reach again.

On the table, a single cup rested on its side, remnants of a milky liquid seeped from the lip. Stepping from the tabletop may have easily toppled the glass.

I tapped my fingers along my canvas breeches. They still bore hints of rose oil and lavender from Brew-Tea-Full. The aromas seemed out of place in this house. Too specific, too different from the mundane decor.

"Why am I here, Leof?" I didn't turn back toward the men. I watched the dead guy in front of me, his vacant eyes pointing over my head. The dark stain of a dagger on his wrist made mine itch, and I resisted the urge to scratch my skin.

The bodies have always been my least favorite part of the job, back in the capital and here in Hallow's Promise.

Castor snorted. "Yeah, *sir*. Why's she here?"

"Just tell me anything you can, Rae. Then I'll take you home."

I glanced over my shoulder, making eye contact with the wolf. I could almost feel the comfort of my little cottage already. "He didn't live here, not permanently at least. There are no personal effects, no evidence of horses or transportation outside, and none of the candles have been lit. He either arrived today or was hiding his presence for some reason."

Castor raised his brow and glanced around the home as though he hadn't seen it before. He snapped his gaze back at me, eyes widening slightly.

I'd surprised him. I reveled in the glee for a moment.

"He has the mark of a Provider, so he probably served the capital at some point or another, but he may not anymore." I shrugged. "I have no way of knowing that. But Leof . . . this looks like a suicide. There's no blood, no sign of a break-in or struggle. He was probably going through a personal issue and didn't know where to find a way out." Heck, I'd been in a dark place after I'd escaped the capital, too. Luckily, I'd found the right things to pull me back out.

I swallowed thickly. It was hard to imagine how dark the world could look until you're back in the light.

Leof ran a hand over his face, but I glimpsed his tight expression. These weren't the words he wanted me to say. I turned away. Watching him only made my guilt worse.

The dead guy kept staring, seeing well beyond our world. The coiled rope sunk deep into his neck. One severed edge protruded from the top of the knot, leaning toward the left side.

Leof started talking again, but I didn't hear him. I glanced around for a chair or stool but hesitated before moving furniture at the scene. Important clues often hid in unexpected places.

"Give me a boost," I said.

The wolf froze mid-sentence. His brow pinched, but he stepped toward me, anyway.

Castor pushed between us.

"She's not touching the body," he growled.

I rolled my eyes.

The constable gestured toward me. "She doesn't have any qualifications. It's obviously a suicide, and you don't want to admit it because you're in hot water after your last screw up."

Leof's fist clenched. A hint of gold stained his eyes as the wolf peeked out. He had too much control to shift unwillingly, but potent emotions brought a shifter's animal to the forefront. He may not go full wolf-out in the middle of a crime scene, but he'd likely throw a few punches. If he was in trouble at work, I didn't want to cause more issues. I actually liked Leof—most of the time.

Also, I wanted to go home.

I let a coil of my magic untwist from inside me. It wanted to yawn, curl up, and go back to sleep. I fed it more energy until it pulsed through me, highlighted my nerves, and itched to seep from my skin.

A single wisp of power pressed forward, and I plucked it from the rest. It twisted as I pulled from inside myself and fed it into the room.

"ENOUGH!"

I didn't open my mouth, though the magic used my voice. The sound etched through the room, punctured the stone floors of the house, and rumbled into the ground. The walls shook. Everyone covered their ears, Leof hunching over with his supersensitive hearing, and the horses neighed outside.

I let the power fade again.

Castor's eyes widened as he turned to me. "What the hell was that?"

"I said, give me a boost." I ignored the question, pointing my response toward Leof instead.

When the wolf stepped forward, Castor remained quiet this time. Good choice.

Leof wrapped his hands around my waist and hoisted me up to the body. I ignored the half sweet, half sickly smell already oozing from the decaying flesh. It wasn't the poor guy's fault he'd bitten the dust.

The knot *did* loop to the left, exactly the way I'd seen it from below. The severed edges of the protrusion clarified from this angle. A dull blade had hacked the rope haphazardly, threads cut at different lengths and consistencies.

The victim's head tilted to the side. A swatch of thick, dark brown hair covered the majority of his face, but his chin looked mostly square. The deep bruise on the side of his neck caught my attention. It poked from below the collar of his tunic. Crisp, white cotton so stark against such a dark purple wound. The semi-circular shape looked familiar, but the size confused me. I couldn't picture any weapon small enough to make such a mark.

"You can put me down now," I said slowly, mind spinning as I put the pieces together—the pieces that I desperately did not want to connect.

My feet touched the ground. Leof stepped back, that half-smirk returning. He'd seen the look enough times to recognize my expression.

"It's not a suicide," he said.

"I can't say that." The methods of crime scene investigations prohibited the use of absolutes. "But the only way the victim tied the knot is if he was left-handed. Right hand dominant users would have the knot on the other side." There, simple, true, and not definite at all.

Castor dropped his head as I snatched the dead man's right hand, ignoring the unearthly hardness of his cold flesh. I turned the palm up into the light. Bands of callouses clustered at the base of each finger with a thicker one settled near the webbing of the thumb.

I grabbed the next hand before the constable stopped me. Please let there be callouses here, too.

Nothing. The skin was smooth, unblemished.

Castor made a low noise and reached toward me. I stepped back before he made contact, thoughts spinning in a direction I didn't want to admit: that it was unlikely the man was left-handed with so many callouses on the other hand.

I hesitated. Bringing up the callouses and bruise would open the opportunity for more questions. I wanted to take a bath and finish brewing up the spell bases for tomorrow's sales.

But I had an obligation, if not to the world, then to Leof. He'd given me so much.

"When you cut the body down, scent map the wound on his neck." Everyone had an individual scent, and a werewolf's developed nose might siphon out specific scents to their owners. It wasn't a perfect science. A lot depended on the time an individual spent near a certain location, how concentrated the scent was, and the amount of time that had passed. Any potential killer's scent would be diluted through the house and smothered by the numerous people inside it. But there may have been enough contact for the bruise to retain some of the scent.

The marshal's brows raised. "Wound?"

I rubbed my palms on my breeches. "It's a bruise, I think. Small, circular, some type of pattern impression. It was hard to see. Do a scent-check and see if anyone beside the victim touched that spot."

Leof nodded. "Will do. Thanks, Rae. Is there anything I can do to repay you?"

"You can take me home."

I headed toward the door, letting Castor and the dead man in the rafters fade behind me. I didn't look back. I didn't need to.

Castor's voice followed us out. "A witch. Nobody told me she was a damn witch."

It wasn't exactly right, but I didn't turn back to correct him.

Chapter 3

Cherry greeted us as we approached, searching our hands for any treats we may have brought from the house. I gave her an apologetic look and patted her cheek in consolation. She shook her head but rubbed her velvet nose on my hand, anyway.

Castor stopped next to us and studied me, from my shoes to the top of my head. From any other man, it may have felt inappropriate, but he had the glowering eyes of a constable searching for a broken law.

A second constable approached us. His softened jawline and smooth brow suggested he was younger, perhaps a rookie to the guard. Castor shifted as he approached but said nothing. An awkward silence hung around the four of us.

The new person stuck out his hand. "Name's Gerrin."

I wrapped my fingers around his. "Rae."

Gerrin stood straighter and cast me a perfect smile. "And who are you, Rae?"

"I'm nobody," I answered honestly. "I sell potions from my wagon and keep my head down whenever this guy lets me." I jerked a thumb toward Leof.

"A potion wagon?" Gerrin's eyes lit. "I think I know that one. It's got a really clever name, right?"

I smiled, "Brew-Tea-Ful."

"That's the one! I got tea there once. An iced juniper berry, with something else mixed in. It tasted wonderful."

I didn't remember every customer, of course, but he looked a little familiar. That specific tea provided courage, antioxidants, and soothed nightmares, so it was a popular choice.

"Thank you," I said.

His brow creased. "What brings you to our crime scene?"

"She's a witch," Castor said before Leof or I answered.

"A witch? You're doing a magic-cast then? For a suicide?"

I pressed my lips together. Gerrin's question reignited Castor's curiosity because both constables stared at me. A magic-cast captured a physical outline of a witch's power if spellwork were involved in a crime. Suspects would be asked, or forced, to use magic so a comparison cast could be made. Similar to fingerprints, every magic user had a distinct impression of their traits. If the casts matched, they could apprehend a suspect.

"I've done some investigations in the past," I answered. Not exactly a lie, but not exactly the truth. The truth was, I'd been intimate with death for far too long and learned more than I desired. "The marshal thought I could offer a different perspective."

Castor rolled his eyes and opened his mouth, then froze.

Leof shot up his hand and stilled. The amber tint in his iris returned as he called the wolf to the surface. All three guards pivoted their attention toward the depths of the forest, an eerie tension drawn over them.

I held my breath and leaned around Leof's thick shoulders. They hadn't drawn any blades yet, thankfully, but their hands twitched toward their sheaths.

The lightest sound of a crunching branch echoed around us. The three men unsheathed their weapons in unison. Leof tried to signal to the other constables lingering near the door, but they didn't look.

"I don't want to yell in case it's the murderer returning to the scene. It might spook them," Leof whispered to me. "Go behind the horse and stay there."

I swallowed at the thought of hiding behind Cherry if something, or someone, terrible exited the woods and tried to harm us. But I scooted along her side, offering comforting pats, until I figured Leof had enough room for . . . whatever he planned.

More sticks crunched. Leaves rustled from the shrubs nearest us.

The others finally noticed the disruption and neared the darkened forest edge beside Leof, Castor, and Gerrin. Unmistakable sounds of branches snapping and leaves scratching rang through the night. The tension turned thick, palpable.

"Come out, now!" Leof yelled.

The movement stopped. Everyone drew a breath—me included. The rest of the forest responded to Leof's shout with sudden stillness.

Leaves crackled again as a creature sprawled from the shrubs. Its round body tipped slightly to one side, propelled by giant rear legs disproportionate to the rest of its mass. The guards staggered back, and I knew why when an unpleasant scent followed the creature's wake.

It paused at the commotion, barely able to lift beady eyes above our ankles. Its giant tongue dashed between non-existent lips and exposed sharpened, ragged teeth. The moist tongue ran over both eyes until the black filament shined with moisture.

"It's a warplog," I said.

Most of the guards dispersed with a groan, hands covering their noses. Castor, Gerrin, and Leof slid closer to me. The warplog leaped toward them and the trio yelped.

"It's harmless." I rolled my eyes. "Although you may want to close the front door. If he's scenting the body, it'll be relentless until it finds it." Then devours the whole thing in a single sitting.

As though it recognized my voice, the warplog turned to me. It resembled a terrible cross between a frog and a rabbit, with the amphibian shape and skin, but muscular hind legs and tiny forearms in front. Our eyes locked, and part of me reached toward the creature in a type of distant kinship. The warplog and I weren't that different—we both managed death and tried to protect others from the harsh realities of it. Me by assisting with death investigations, and the warplog by eliminating decomposing bodies which may spread disease.

Gerrin shied further away from it. "They found a warplog by my brother's body in Erline." I flinched at the true name of the capital. It was rarely used, for rumors said the king may hear the word anywhere in the world. Gerrin's eyes turned glossy. "They had to rip his bones from its mouth to recover all the pieces."

His words met silence. I pressed my lips together, unsure of what to say, and Leof caught my gaze with a similar expression.

"I'm sorry for your loss," I said, since the other men seemed content to let the awkward silence stew. "But the warplog should be relocated before it tries to eat the victim."

Gerrin remained quiet for a moment. "We should kill it."

He took two steps toward the warplog before I processed his words. The silver of his blade reflected the few lanterns the guards had set up. The warplog's dark stare followed the metal curiously.

"Wait." I grabbed Gerrin's wrist without realizing I'd moved. He froze beneath me, his muscles tensed. "It's harmless, and it didn't do anything."

"It ate my brother," he said. "And it'll eat this body, too."

I gently tightened my grip and raised his blade. I covered his fingers with my other hand and let a brush of my power flow through us. Using more than the barest of my power risked my safety—which was why I turned to potions to strengthen and distribute the magic—but a slight amount soothed the constable's heart and breathing.

"*This* warplog didn't eat your brother, I promise." I pried the blade from his grasp. He let it fall into my hand, and I passed it to Leof. "I'll take this one and move it. He doesn't deserve to die for his nature."

I looked back at the creature. Its tongue dashed out and licked its eyeballs again. I was surprised nature hadn't killed this one off yet.

Gerrin stepped back. The blank expression slipped from his face and that good-natured smile returned. He winked at me.

"Go ahead, if you can stand the smell."

I scooped the warplog into my arms and it settled its head on my forearm with a sense of entitlement. Its long legs relaxed, and those beady eyes closed. I wrinkled my nose at the scent, but the creature dozed almost immediately.

"Alright Leof, take us home."

He raised a brow. "With that stench the entire way?"

"I'm not sure if you or the warplog smell worse. Now shut up and get on the horse."

The werewolf chuckled, but hopped into the saddle.

***

The warplog's scent weakened as we rode, making the evening ride almost enjoyable. Leof made a great companion and only spoke when he had something to say.

I studied the woods while my smaller companion's breaths pushed against my arms. Tree trunks fought against gravity to claim the most sunlight during these warmer months. Brown needles dripped from heavy limbs and fell into the piles of pinecones and debris. Cherry's hooves broke green needles and released a sharp forest scent through the air. Scatterings of mushrooms and wildflowers sprouted where the trees hadn't barricaded yet.

But the forest held more than foliage. Nothing moved within it, but the darkness clung a little tighter in shadowed spaces. Vague outlines formed and dissipated.

My cottage nestled in a rounded clearing on the West Brim of Hallow's Promise, near the city wall. I had a neighbor on each side, which helped ward away some of the darkest parts of the forest. The wooden house had been built long before I'd fled the capital and would likely remain after I left. I had newer windows installed and the crystalline glass glowed with the fire that ignited itself at sunset each night.

Brew-Tea-Ful perched to the right of the front door. No wheel or hoof prints lined the powdered dirt before it. Leof likely wouldn't have noticed, but I saw a slight shake as Brew greeted me.

The wolf stopped Cherry at the little stepstone walkway that led from the road to my door. He squinted at the wagon.

"How'd it get here?"

I slipped off the horse, careful not to wake my sleepy passenger, and smiled. "Goodnight, Leof."

I headed toward the door.

"You know, one of these days you're going to have to tell me some of your secrets," he called after me.

"They'll send someone from the capital to investigate this death." I kept my gaze down as I climbed the two steps to my door.

Leof's voice came out soft. "You know I would never tell anyone about you."

I didn't answer, instead fished my key from my breeches and popped open the lock. My wards buzzed, alerting me to the open door. My protection magic was rather weak, and the most it could do was buzz like a little alarm if there was a breach to my home.

I turned back to the marshal, who was already headed toward the road.

"Hey, Leof!"

He twisted the reins to turn back toward me. "What?"

"If you have another case, don't find me."

I shut the door, drowning out the wolf's fading chuckle.

Chapter 4

The warplog *did* smell, which wasn't surprising considering decomposing flesh formed its entire diet. I quickly washed and changed clothes after the scene, then bundled some old rags into a nest on the floor in the open living space, and set two pots of water into the fire to warm. One pot for the simple syrups to restock Brew, and another for the warplog's warm bath.

I glanced at my unexpected guest. He had burrowed into the fabric until only his beady eyes peeked through, watching my every move. His tongue dashed out and licked his eye again.

"You make it really hard to defend you," I told him.

He licked the other eye.

I turned back to the fire, adding wood and stoking the coals until the flames licked the centers of the cauldrons. Once heat rose from the smaller pot, I pulled it from the flames. I rummaged through the kitchen cupboards, finding a bowl large enough for the warplog's round body. I added gentle soap and a few drops of lavender oil. The warm water foamed with bubbles as I poured it into the bowl.

I placed the makeshift bathtub onto the ground beside the warplog's nest. He watched, motionless.

"Listen, if you're going to spend the night here, then I need you to smell better. Tomorrow, I can set you free when I can be sure there are no predators nearby. But you need a bath tonight."

He blinked slowly. I sighed. "I'm in desperate need of some conversation if I'm talking to a warplog. What should I call you, anyway?"

One of his thick hind legs lifted and stretched until the clawed toes peered from the rags as well. The creature turned his head and scratched enthusiastically.

I shook my head and stood, leaving the bowl on the floor. He'd either bathe, or he wouldn't, and we both knew I wasn't going to kick him out tonight. Those beady eyes saw right through my bluff.

I washed my hands and brought out the pre-measured sacks of sugar from the kitchen. When eager bubbles burst in the second pot, I dropped the powder in and stirred until it dissolved. A rich, sweet scent enveloped the living room.

The bubbles settled once I removed the cauldron from the flames. I dipped a giant ladle into the liquid and portioned out equal measurements into more bowls. The aromas of herbs and flowers overlapped with the sugar, mixing the cottage in a familiar scent of potion ingredients.

I added lavender into one bowl, a perfect base for simple headaches, anxiety, and sleep disorders. The solution immediately took a purple tint. The next jar I opened released the sharp scent of ginger. It created promising tonics for upset stomachs.

Once I'd added all the herbs into the bases, I covered the bowls with cheesecloth and set them on the ledge near the window to cool. In the morning, I would strain the syrup, leaving only the rich flavors and benefits without the bitter leaves.

These tasks seemed mundane, boring, but I clung to the routine every day. I had known a time when secrets and surprises trailed me, and I didn't long to return to that lifestyle.

Dizziness covered me in a sudden wave. I gripped the edge of the counter and closed my eyes until it passed. I pushed myself too hard tonight. Crime scenes always exhausted me, and I should have gone to bed instead of restocking base tonics. But Brew provided for me. I'd have nothing without it.

I sighed. My mind refused to quiet after everything today.

Another Provider in Hallow's Promise meant trouble. The capital would send someone to investigate. They were too valuable. If I were smart, I would flee until this passed over. If I were really smart, I'd move to a new town and start over again.

But I didn't want to. I'd worked hard to build a life in Hallow's Promise. It wasn't the grand city of the capital, but it contained far more beauty. The people here didn't hide behind masks, didn't flaunt their success over the suffering of others.

They didn't abuse people for their powers.

A sharp pain radiated up my jaw, and I released my clenched teeth. I took a deep breath until the edge of panic faded.

I wouldn't leave—because I didn't want to.

With my mind made up, and my potions seeping for the night, I turned back to the warplog, expecting his dark eyes to be watching through the rags again.

He'd nestled in the bath instead. His round little body almost filled the bowl completely, tipping suds of water over the side. Those beady eyes pressed closed, and I swore he was smiling. A cluster of bubbles perched atop his head like a snowy hat.

I smiled and grabbed a clean towel from a drawer. I kneeled beside the creature and swiped the wad of bubbles from the top of his head.

"Seems fitting for you." I gently scooped him from the cooling water and wrapped him up. He didn't drop the lipless smile from his face, or even open his eyes. "Come on, Bubbles, it's time for bed."

The fire dimmed on its own as I climbed the ladder to the loft overhead. I dragged an old pillow from beneath the bed, placed it on the floor at my side, and settled Bubbles onto it. I thought it would take me a long time to fall asleep as thoughts of bodies and werewolves occupied my mind, but darkness quickly found me.

***

The wards screamed in my head. I jerked upright in bed and grabbed the blade that rested on my nightside table. Its dark metal reminded me of the past, but it was the only weapon in the cottage.

Quiet stretched around us. The warplog released subtle snores, overlapped by the soft crackles of the fire. No hint of a screeching door, no whine of unwelcome horses in the yard.

But something had broken the wards. That mental alarm sounded over and over. Someone had breached the barriers of the house.

I drew a deep breath. It couldn't be a coincidence that a Provider dies in Hallow's Promise; then my wards are broken. My hands shook as I pushed the blankets down and slipped my legs over the edge of the bed. Nothing grabbed my ankle. I took that as a positive sign.

Bubbles didn't move as I eased around his bed. I paused after each step and listened for any hint of an intruder. Only silence and fire.

I gripped the railing at the edge of the loft and peered down. Not even the shadows moved below, but a sliver of moonlight stemmed from a crack in the door. Maybe I'd forgotten to shut it all the way before bed, and the breeze blew it open.

Even thinking the words felt like a lie. I couldn't sleep with an unlocked door since the day I left the capital, and my life became my own for the first time. I had shut and latched the door before climbing the ladder.

I clenched my teeth until my jaw hurt. Going downstairs was a bad idea. But staying up here, like a coward, might be even worse.

If it was someone from the capital, I'd turn the knife to my own heart. Death was better than returning to the king.

The first rung of the ladder pressed against my foot. Coolness replaced the warmth I'd left in bed. I took another step, and another, waiting for the grip of a stranger on my ankle, until I was level with Bubble's sleeping face. At least he'd have a nice meal if I died.

The thought made me swallow.

I continued downward until my feet touched the wooden floor. Shadows hugged the deepest part of the living space beneath the loft, while the low fire illuminated the kitchen with dim light. I didn't want to turn my back to the darkness, but closing the door took priority. The last thing I wanted was for someone to burst through the door while I searched the rest of the house.

My heart caught in my throat as I eased forward. Cool wood met my hand, staining my skin with the chill. I shut it slowly, glancing away from the shadows to watch the latch click in the doorframe. My breath slipped out in relief with the audible snap.

Before I fully looked up again, a shadowed figure of a man lunged at me from beneath the loft. I sucked in air to scream, but he clamped a hand across my mouth and pushed me against the door. In one moment, I watched him rush me. In the next, he had my face pressed against the wood.

The stranger leaned in, an earthy scent caught between us. "This is a pretty blade. Don't mind if I borrow it." He plucked the knife from my hand, and my cheeks heated at how easily he achieved it. A quick flick of his wrist sent my knife tip deep into the floor.

The rough edge of the rope scratched at my skin. He kept one hand on my mouth and wrapped bindings on both of my wrists with the other. I angled to get a layer of his skin between my teeth, but he avoided the attempts effortlessly.

"If you want me in your mouth, all you have to do is ask." His voice was velvet in my ears, lighting a fire of hatred inside my chest. Most Providers received hand-to-hand combat training, eventually becoming an expert to avoid certain death. The king deemed my specific powers too dangerous to learn to fight. I knew he wanted to keep me defenseless in case he ever needed to kill me himself.

Tonight, I cursed him more than ever.

The stranger pressed harder against me. I glimpsed at the side of his face where his brow creased.

"Not fear. Anger. That's surprising," he whispered, almost to himself. He raised his voice, "Do I need to give you the entire speech that if you yell, I'll have to kill you, or are you going to be a good girl?"

'Good girl' had certainly never described me. But the longer he held me against the door and cracked rogue jokes in my ears, the more I doubted he knew who I was. Any Provider searching for me wouldn't mess around with humor. They'd drag me outside and into an iron wagon immediately.

I clenched my jaw but shook my head. A half-smile slipped across his cheek as he removed his hand from my mouth and stepped aside, giving me space to draw a deep breath.

The earthy scent returned, oozing from the stranger like natural cologne.

"What do you want?" I asked over my shoulder, face still pressed against the door.

The man gripped my biceps above the rope restraints he'd tied and turned me into the open room. "Better ask him."

The shadows beneath my loft ripped apart and coughed out a man in a familiar black cloak. I remembered the itch of that fabric on my skin, the pressure as the raised hood set against my hair, the darkness obscuring not only my face, but my view of the world. If he raised his sleeve, his forearm would have the mark of the Provider etched on his skin.

He didn't glance at mine. No, if anything, he looked bored. Some knots deep in my chest untangled a bit. They really hadn't recognized me. They weren't here to drag me back to the king.

Which meant I needed to be very careful to keep it that way.

The robed man dragged his gaze from the top of my head to my toes. His expression remained flat, but the examination made me want to take a bath. He held a thick staff in one hand, exposing his powers as some kind of elemental—which needed contact with the earth to channel magic.

A spark dashed in his eyes, a brief window into his mind. "Kneel."

I raised a brow and opened my mouth, but the Provider tapped his staff on the ground before any unfortunate words left my lips. A coil of thick, black magic wrapped around my legs and forced my knees to bend. Only the other stranger's grip on my arms kept me from face planting into the floor.

"I've been told you were at Provider Hagley's murder." The new Provider's voice stretched each syllable as thick as a strand of maple syrup, but not nearly as sweet.

I bit my tongue. "I wasn't at the actual event."

The man behind me chuckled, and the Provider glared at us both.

"You saw his body?"

"Yes."

"It bore a wound?"

My heart sank a little deeper. I had only told that information to Leof, and Leof would never reveal my existence unless his life depended on it.

Or his daughter's.

"What did you do to him?" My magic threatened to twist with a burst of rage. I needed to reel it in, or he may recognize it—or worse. Using too much of my power sent my location directly to the king.

That spark returned. "The werewolf? Don't worry, he was alive when we left."

I clenched my fists and side-eyed my blade. Could I lunge quickly enough to snatch it and stab the Provider before either man stopped me?

The stranger at my back kneeled beside me. "Don't even think about it."

I blinked. He couldn't possibly know what I had been thinking.

"Normally, we would not concern ourselves with something as mundane as murder," the Provider continued, as though I didn't plot his death in my mind. It was probably an occupational hazard he dealt with regularly. "But the death of a Provider cannot be overlooked."

Or else the king would appear weak, unable to protect those devoted to him.

"What does that have to do with me?" I asked. "I sell tea."

"Ah, yes, we saw the wagon outside. What a peculiar livelihood. It would be such a shame if something were to happen to it, perhaps something similar to what happened to your werewolf friend?"

"What do you want?" I couldn't quite keep my voice level.

"Good, we got here faster than the marshal did. I want you to figure out who murdered the Provider and bring them to me to answer for their crimes."

Bring them to a slow and painful death, he meant.

"I'm not a marshal," I said. "I don't know anything about solving a crime like this."

The Provider shrugged. "You can bring me the culprit, or you can take his place. I think the decision is easy, but you may disagree."

"Why does the capital even care? Providers die all the time." Anger turned my words bold. The sharpness of my tongue bordered on treason, to imply the king didn't protect his people—though more often he killed them himself.

The Provider's glare narrowed. He pushed his hood back, revealing an oval face with a sharp chin. Worry lines hugged the corner of his eyes and the very center of his forehead. A gray tint stained his dark brown eyes, a dimness from seeing far too much horror in the world.

"Someone in your position should choose their words more carefully." An echo followed his warning, three hollow whispers spoken in unison.

I quieted. As much as I hated it, these strangers had the upper hand. I was unarmed and outmatched. If they'd been able to hurt Leof, killing me would be child's play.

"Ah, I see you do have *some* intelligence. Let me make this perfectly clear. I refuse to stay in a town of such low standards." The Provider curled his lip and side-eyed my cottage. "So, I will leave you in Mr. Valen's tender care. He will remain here to . . . assist in the investigation. And I will return in a fortnight, either for the culprit—or for you."

Assist, meaning watching my every move.

He opened his mouth to say more, but a loud thump echoed from upstairs. The man holding me—Valen—jerked his gaze to the loft ladder. The Provider raised his staff.

Another thump echoed, and another. Two shimmering, dark eyes peered over the opening for the ladder and a sliver of pink escaped the shadows as Bubbles' tongue dashed over their surface.

I closed my eyes and took a deep breath. "It's a warplog." A hint of an apology stained my voice. "He's harmless."

Valen raised a thick brow. "They're anything but harmless."

Bubbles raised onto his embarrassingly short forelegs and peered over the loft. His muscles tensed a moment before those thick back legs hopped him right over the edge. One long toe on his back foot caught the rung of the ladder and he tumbled down with a throaty groan, landing in a greenish heap on his back.

His upside-down gaze locked on me, and he licked his eyes again.

The Provider raised a lip. "One more moment in this stye is too long." He started toward the door, barely looking at me again. "Fourteen days, girl, and I'll be back. Don't forget."

Valen stood, sent me a wink, and followed the Provider. The door shut with a final click.

Silence beat through the house for a blissful moment. I twisted my wrists and found the restraints slipped off easily with the right amount of tension.

My thoughts spun as the adrenaline crash stirred nausea in my gut. I needed to get up and check on Leof and Suzie. Then, I would pack all the supplies that fit inside Brew and get the hell out of Hallow's Promise. If I left quickly, Valen wouldn't have time to stop me. After I'd fled, the king would have appointed the best trackers to search for me. If they hadn't found me, this random goon wouldn't either.

Bubbles groaned again. He flipped onto his stomach, sucked in a deep breath, and stretched his mouth. The gaping hole opened wider and wider and wider until those fleshless lips pulled taunt enough to devour an entire man in one swallow. Sharp, razor teeth lined his top and bottom jaws. Oozing green saliva dripped into a puddle on my floor and bubbled at the edges.

I didn't have enough energy to be shocked. The night's events stole even that from me.

"Too late, Bub." I pushed from the ground, grabbed my shoes, and pulled open the front door. First, check on Leof and Suzie. "Way too late."

Then, get the hell out of Hallow's Promise.

Chapter 5

By the time I reached Brew, I realized I'd left my only weapon stabbed in the floorboards inside. I silently cursed, but didn't turn back for it. The knife hadn't helped me against the Provider and Valen.

Wood, much warmer than the evening should have allowed, met against my palm. A pulse of the wagon's power surged through me, partially mine, and partially its own.

"I know, I know," I said. "We're leaving tonight, but I have to check on Leof and Suzie first."

Strong magic whisked around me, and I closed my eyes, letting Brew take us as close to Leof's as possible. The world slipped beneath my feet and reappeared before I had time to lose my balance.

Leof lived in the heart of Hallow's Promise, in a large house with the marshal's symbol—an eagle with outstretched wings—pinned on the front door. Similar houses surrounded his, framed by clusters of pruned trees and ponds with bubbling waterfalls. A few others held status symbols on their doors as well, but their windows remained darkened at this time of night, and Leof's house glowed with lanterns from inside.

"Stay here," I told Brew, with a gentle pat as I headed for Leof's home. The wagon sent a few warning creaks my way.

Two stairs climbed to a short, raised porch. Thick, white curtains blocked the windows except for the warm glow of the lanterns. Muffled voices slipped from inside. I rapped my fist twice on the door, and they stopped.

The curtains ruffled slightly, though I didn't see anyone look through. The door cracked a moment later and Suzie's round face appeared, along with the scent of cinnamon and fire, followed by the metallic tinge of blood.

Her eyes narrowed. "You shouldn't be here."

"I wanted to check on your dad."

"You're the reason they hurt him. You should go." Suzie tried to shut the door as a deeper voice sounded within.

I put my foot in the crack. "You don't understand what happened, who these people are. I need to talk to your father."

A bite of power sparked in the air. Suzie's eyes turned amber. I'd never learned if she shared an animal like her father, or if something else came from her mother, but I didn't want to find out.

Heavy footsteps echoed. Leof's fingers curled around the door and pulled it from his daughter's hands. She stepped back, openly scowling.

"I told you to let her in." The marshal's voice sounded quieter than I'd ever heard. He stood upright, but stooped over, clad in only loose-fitting breeches. Specks of dark brown clung to his pants, soaking into the waistline.

I stepped inside the house and took the door from Leof's hand, slowly closing it.

"What did they do?" I asked.

The werewolf grimaced. "I'm sorry, Rae. I told them everything I could without mentioning you, but they knew someone else was involved. I promise I wouldn't have told them, but they started threatening Suzie . . ."

She rolled her eyes, which had faded to a normal dark color. "I can take care of myself."

Leof staggered. We both lunged toward him, catching his frame before he sagged to the ground.

"Let's get him back on the couch." Suzie and I half carried, half dragged Leof through the house. Glowing lanterns cast our shadows on the walls, larger than life and more powerful than I felt. Several scented candles revealed where the cinnamon smell originated. Most of the furniture remained simple, offering hardly more than the basic comforts. A linen couch centered in a large family room, already covered in rivets of blood.

Suzie and I placed Leof face down on the cushions, and he groaned. I stepped back and bit my tongue to avoid cursing.

Ragged lines slashed across the werewolf's back, as though giant talons sliced through skin and muscle alike. Blood oozed with each breath the man took. Sweat peppered his skin, combining with the red fluid to create a gory, vivid paint.

"What did they do?"

"The robed guy smashed his staff on the ground, and dad started screaming." Suzie's eyes glazed over, wrapped in the recent past. "Every time he refused to answer a question, the man did it again and again." She glanced at me. "Until he finally mentioned you."

I pressed my lips. "Why won't it heal?"

"We don't know."

"I'll be fine," Leof said, muffled by the couch fabric. "Magical wounds take longer to heal."

"Suzie, can you get me some damp rags?" I asked.

She narrowed her gaze again. "You're trying to get rid of me. I'm not leaving you alone with dad. This is your fault, too."

I didn't answer. She wasn't wrong.

"Suzie, just go. I'll be fine," Leof said.

She rolled her eyes and stomped into the depths of the house.

I kneeled by Leof's head and lowered my voice. "You and Suzie need to pack up and leave tonight. These people are ruthless, and if they find out who I am, everyone I know will be in danger—including you."

His jaw clenched as he raised his head to study my face. "And who are you, Rae? I don't know what to be careful about because you've never trusted me with your past."

"My past doesn't matter." Trusting anyone only put them in more danger. "But do not expect mercy from the king's Provider. I don't know who the second man is, but I guarantee neither would hesitate to free your guts from your skin if they realized you'd help hide me all these years."

His gaze softened. A sweaty lock of brown hair fell across his forehead. "Are you leaving?"

I hesitated, then nodded. "It's the only safe thing for you, too."

"You know I can't just walk out of Hallow's Promise, Rae. I'm not like you. I have a life here. Suzie has a life here. She deserves to see her mom, too, and I can't choose between taking that away or leaving her behind. My work impacts my community. I want to help these people, Rae, they're my friends."

I sat back on my heels. His words felt like slaps across my face. Of course, it was easy for me to leave; I'd never let anyone get to know me. I didn't have any friends to miss me.

"You don't understand. These people would tear you apart."

He shrugged. "I'll give my last breath to ward them off, but some things, some people, are worth dying for."

"Look at you!" I hissed through clenched teeth. "This is nothing compared to what that Provider can do! He'd leave you shredded and turn to whoever else may have known I existed. Is that what you want?"

Silence beat around us. The crackling fire muted only by Leof's labored breathing.

"And what do you want, Rae? To be alone again? To live in fear for the rest of your life? Find me when you have those answers, then I'll tell you what I want."

I wanted to be angry, but exhaustion numbed me. I wouldn't be able to convince the werewolf to leave. Once the Provider learned I'd disobeyed his orders and ran, he would slaughter Leof just to prove a point. Maybe Suzie, too—maybe the whole town.

The numbness spread.

"Let me get you something for the pain," I said.

Leof protested, but I retreated to the front door, shut it behind me, and walked across the cobblestone street in the bitter moonlight to Brew-Tea-Ful. The wagon eagerly opened the doors before I touched its frame.

Soft tea-light candles illuminated the space as I worked. I set the kettle filled with water on the small stovetop, which already glowed hot with flames.

If I left Hallow's Promise, they would hunt Leof down, I was sure of it. Not because I believed he couldn't solve the murder—I knew he could—but because Providers didn't allow offenses to go unpunished. When he discovered my offense of fleeing, Leof would bear my punishment.

The kettle started screeching, and I lifted it from the flames to rest on the countertop. I spooned some loose-leaf meadowsweet tea into the water, sniffing the sweet floral aroma, and adding a bit more until the scent turned rich.

Remaining in Hallow's Promise risked being dragged into everything I'd run from at the capital. The king couldn't kill me without losing access to my powers, but he'd make my life miserable until I wished for death.

I poured a healthy amount of milk into a metal cup. Brew fluttered opened several cabinets, and I pulled out the turmeric and dandelion root oil. The milk turned a sharp orange color, and I whisked it until frothy bubbles formed.

Leaving would preserve my life.

It would end Leof's.

He'd asked me what I wanted. Truthfully, I didn't know, but I knew it wasn't more death at my hands.

I grabbed a werewolf sized mug and strained the meadowsweet tea just above halfway. The milk froth poured thickly on top, herby and sweet mixing together. The pale yellow and deep orange merged, exposing a golden color of the morning sun.

I stared at the mug.

Either choice risked losing this life I'd built. I only got to decide how my future would change now.

I cradled the mug in both hands, stepped over the cobblestones, and slipped back inside Leof's home.

Suzie sat on the floor beside her father. I set the mug on a short table near the couch.

"This will help with the pain, and to prevent infection," I said. "Send word if you need more, or if the wounds get worse." I turned away.

"Will you be home?" Leof asked, pain thick in his words.

Home? I wasn't sure what that word even meant.

"Yeah," I heard myself answer. "I'll be home."

I guess I had a friend, after all, and I didn't want to see him die.

Chapter 6

"You have to go home now." Most people would feel silly talking to a warplog in the crisp moments before dawn, when the air promises winter's arrival soon. I didn't have any pride left. Running on very little sleep and too much adrenaline, I longed to crawl back into bed. But moping didn't make money, and it certainly didn't solve murders.

Bubbles licked his eyeball. I sighed and pressed my palm against my eyes.

"Fine, you don't have to hop away, but you can't just sit out here. Something will eat you." He didn't appear concerned with his impending doom. "Let's go."

I scooped the warplog into my arms, and he settled his head in the crook of my elbow. He let his long hind legs fall limp, and soft snores almost immediately filtered through his lipless mouth.

"I don't know how you even survived in the wild," I mumbled, dashing inside to grab a towel before carrying my cargo out to Brew.

The wards pulsed as I closed the door. It felt pointless to set them—a Provider had already found me—but old habits die hard.

The wagon's rear door fluttered open as we approached. I gave its frame a pat as we stepped inside.

"You need to be away from the ingredients, so you'll have to stay in this cupboard, but I can leave the door open." I orchestrated the towel into a neat little bed and set Bub in the center. He lazily opened one eye, flicked his leg a couple times, and went back to snoring.

A vibration hummed beneath my feet as Brew prepared to take us to our usual destination.

But today wasn't usual. We had a murder to solve.

"We're not going to the college." I stocked the new syrups as I spoke. The normal routine felt too mundane. Part of me expected the Provider to show up, reveal my secret identity, and drag me away to the king. I'd always imagined I'd be doing something far more exhilarating than stocking shelves when that happened. "We have to solve the stranger's murder if we want the Provider to leave without asking too many questions about me. It's possible the killer frequents that area, or neighbors witnessed something they didn't find suspicious at the time, so we need to get as close to the crime scene as possible, but not be too obvious."

The vibrations stopped.

"Look," I told the wagon, the second time this morning I was arguing with something that couldn't speak back to me. Maybe my personal line for sanity was dwindling. "I'm not a marshal, but I am a potions-maker. Even if I can't solve this case, I can certainly sell some drinks. And that's what we're going to do."

Draws clicked open and shut in what I figured meant Brew laughed at me. But the back door latched, the world narrowed and twisted, then steadied a heartbeat later.

"Thank you," I said.

Fresh sunlight streamed through the side window as I drew the sash up. I let the morning greet me while I placed a chalkboard outside displaying a list of all my offered drinks, and a note that I could make custom potions upon request. The intersection was near the town's gate, potentially a good location for daytime travelers and merchants. Hopefully, I could make a little money to restock the frozen drawer and possibly find some clues for this case.

***

"One of these can help me stay awake?" The short, blonde woman squinted skeptically at my menu. Brew and I preferred our usual spots, and it had been long enough since we'd tried a new sales location I'd forgotten how mistrusting people started out. Her skepticism didn't discourage me, though, since several other travelers lined up behind her.

"I'd recommend the Lion's Paw. It's a little earthy, but I can add some extra sweetener to balance the flavor. It's guaranteed to keep your energy high all day." I smiled. The poor woman harbored dark circles under her eyes, and she swayed on her feet. She could use warm, regenerating tea.

"Alright." Her tone did not sound confident. "I guess I'll try it."

Brew flung open the cup cupboard, and I grabbed a tall mug. The water remained at a light boil on the small oven. Steam rose as I poured some into the mug before topping off the cauldron on the flame again. The mug heated to a comforting temperature, and I spooned the mushroom tea in to steep.

"Are you visiting Hallow's Promise, or just passing through?" I took the simple syrup off the shelf, measured a healthy amount into a small pot, and set it on the stove to boil.

She watched every move with one brow lifted. "Oh, I'm just passing through. I wanted to stay the night, but I've heard the area hasn't been kind to visitors lately."

I smothered a surprised expression. As soft boiling pops began in the simple syrup, I spooned an additional helping of sugar into the mixture. The added sweetness would soften the earthy citrus tones of the mushroom tea and give the customer a quick burst of energy while the benefits of the herbs absorbed more slowly.

"What do you mean by that? There's plenty of travelers in Hallow's Promise."

She shrugged. "Rumors say it's best to avoid staying here, at least for longer visits." She leaned into the window. "I've heard someone tried to move here and got run out of town. It's only a rumor, but as a single traveler, it was enough to scare me from it."

"Hm." I pulled a second mug from the cupboard and strained the tea into it. The simple syrup disappeared into the golden liquid, and I gave it a quick stir. Sweet and mellow scents combined, already elevating my mood.

The customer's eyes lit up. "Oh, that smells good!"

She gave me her coins, and I passed the mug through the sash. She cradled it in both hands, inhaling sharply, barely touching the tea to her lips. I caught the edge of a smile before she disappeared.

I turned to the next customer, a shorter woman with her light hair wrapped in twin braids framing a soft, round face.

"I'll be just a moment to prepare for your order."

Bub snored softly from his towel bed in the cupboard as I rinsed the mug in the basin and set it to dry. A light wind bustled through the wagon, helping the water drops evaporate. I stoked the fire and added kindling to keep the water hot.

I mused over the previous customer's words while I worked. I hadn't heard any rumors about danger at Hallow's Promise, but I certainly avoided travel at all costs. And most people. I didn't know what may have happened to a couple attempting to move here, and I didn't know where to find out.

I'd just started investigating and was already stuck.

Grinding my teeth, I turned back to the window. "How can I help you?"

She opened her mouth, her gaze dashed to the side, and she paused.

Her eyes widened.

A dark shadow fell across the woman's face, growing larger as its owner approached, until the shadow engulfed the petite woman. She didn't look afraid, though. Actually, her mouth propped open, a pink blush covered her cheeks, and her brows disappeared into her parted hairline.

"Excuse me," a deep, terribly familiar voice purred out of sight from my window. "I need a moment with the brewer."

It was undoubtedly the man who'd assisted the Provider with breaking into my house and threatening me last night. That low rumble he'd whispered in my ear would be permanently marked in my memories.

Valen.

Bubble's eyes cracked open at the sound, like he recognized it, too.

The customer didn't protest, and the shadow stepped from the sunlight to stand at my window.

Oh my. I knew why the woman stared speechless now. The man was far more attractive than he'd appeared when breaking and entering into my home in the middle of the night. Muscles lined his frame, turning his body thick but lean. The midnight darkness had hidden his slightly squared chin at the bottom of a sharp jawline. A perfect, straight nose grounded his face, with thick brows framing lovely blue eyes. I knew taking that simple, dark tunic off would reveal a sculpted body beneath.

And I hated him.

Flames ate me from the inside out, and not because of his attractiveness. At least, not only that. He represented the physical embodiment of where my life had altered. He'd held me helpless and defenseless inside my home. Those full lips may beg to be kissed, but I'd just as soon carve them from his face.

"What do you want?" I asked, the words hotter than the water boiling beside me.

He *smirked*. "Good morning to you too, Sunshine."

"My name is Rae."

"Isn't that what I said?" He winked at me.

I'd never wanted to slap anyone more. Even my anger against the king for the years of servitude he'd forced upon me had hardened and frozen into something much colder. This man was a match, one I wished to watch engulf in flames.

"What. Do. You. Want."

He leaned inside the window and glanced around. "This is an interesting way to solve a murder. Can't say I've ever gotten a confession from offering someone a drink."

"I told you last night, I'm not a marshal."

"And you were told that didn't matter." His tone sounded light, but the threat was real.

Bubs shifted in his cupboard, licking his eyes, and flicking his back legs. He didn't like Valen either.

Valen glanced at the menu. "Do you have anything for a good time?"

He winked *again*.

I made my smile so sweet it would rival the concentrated syrup I'd just mixed.

"I have the perfect thing for you." I knocked twice on Brew's counter and a drawer popped open at the back of the wagon. A lone, pale pink flower perched neatly inside. I carefully carried it to the window.

"Why don't you give this a try, *Val*," I said.

Valen considered the oleander for a moment. He glanced back at me. A darker expression stained his face—consideration and perhaps a bit of a challenge. "I'd better not."

I put the bud down and a breeze knocked it toward the floor, where a short trash receptacle conveniently caught the toxic bloom.

"Why are you really here?"

"I'm here to watch you, as the Provider instructed."

I glanced at his wrist. "You're not marked."

His upper lip curled, exposing white teeth. "I'm not one of them."

Curious. His reaction sounded unexpectedly hostile.

"But you're working with one?" I asked.

"I'm working *for* one," he clarified. "They're paying me—handsomely."

"A mercenary, then." I rolled my eyes. That made sense. His muscular physique and ease of apprehending me supported the title.

That smooth smile returned. "I prefer the term 'consultant.'"

"And I prefer the term assho—"

Another voice interrupted me.

"Excuse me. So, so sorry to interfere, but I was wondering if you were actually planning on ordering a drink, or if you were going to harass the hostess all day?"

We both paused and slowly looked over Valen's shoulder where the question originated.

The petite blonde woman crossed her arms and stared the mercenary down. The blush and starry-eyed expression had faded, replaced with a stern, no-nonsense glare. I did a double take. She wore an oversized tunic dyed with several colors that stopped below her knees. White breeches peeked from beneath, tucked into high leather boots with a cord crisscrossing them shut. Scraps of colored fabric tied the ends of her twin braids.

"Harass?" Valen squinted, then let the smile return. "I see I've been put in my place for now. I'd hate to hold up any more of your lovely customers. I'll be sure to check in later."

He gave me a mocking bow, chuckled as I rolled my eyes again, and sulked away to wherever he had come from.

Tension loosened in my chest, and I drew in a deep breath.

"Some men, I swear." The woman stepped forward, still watching where Valen had disappeared. "Is he going to be a problem? Do you need someone to help you?"

"Do you know anyone?" I asked.

"I meant me."

I didn't reveal that her words made me smile. The fierceness in her eyes said she wouldn't appreciate it. And the offer was kind, which seemed to be rare these days. But involving anyone else in my situation also put their life at risk, and—despite irritating a very intimidating mercenary—I didn't want anyone to die, including me.

I sighed. "I think I'll be okay." Though the words tasted false. "What can I get for you?"

She leaned in close and lowered her voice. I was tired of people doing that.

"What I really want is to help you solve the murder."

Chapter 7

I tried to keep my expression blank. "What murder?"

"The murder the intimidating man mentioned. He said, 'Can't say I've ever gotten a confession from offering someone a drink.' I assumed anything less than murder didn't deserve such threats."

Her wide, chocolate brown eyes furrowed with intensity. Intelligence burned beneath the curiosity. Lying to her would make her dig more.

She didn't wait for me to answer. "Was it the murder just down the street from here?" She tilted her head and pondered the Brew-Tea-Ful sign. "I bet that's why you're selling here today. I've seen you at the college, but not at this part of town. You wanted to see if the killer would show up here."

"I-what-how do you know all this?" It was my turn to lean closer. "How do you know about the murder?"

"Everyone over here knows about it. The sheriff's office blocked half the roads for the whole night. They kept calling it a suicide, but why would they send out a marshal? Oh my gosh, were you there, too? I bet I saw you there. I watched them for hours. They cleared out almost the entire house."

She drew a deep breath and stared at me.

Words fumbled in my mouth but refused to leave.

"Oh, I'm sorry, I did it again. I tend to ramble when I'm excited. The point is, I know there was a murder and now some guy is threatening you, and I want in."

My thoughts finally connected enough to form coherent words. "Trust me, you do not want to be involved in this."

"I sure do. Nothing ever happens in Hallow's Promise. I'm not going to sit down and watch when something finally does."

The fact that nothing ever happens in Hallow's Promise was exactly why I'd fled here five years ago. Times seemed to change.

"There are dangerous people interested in this potential crime. You could get hurt."

Her eyes flashed. "I can take care of myself. The first customer said that traveling through the town wasn't safe right now, and another couple had been driven out. I bet the best person to ask about travelers would be the gate guards at the wall. We should go there now and interrogate them!"

Damn, that was a good idea, and one I hadn't considered. The gate guards would know who came and left recently, and if traveling posed any recent dangers. I needed to talk to them as soon as I finished selling today.

"What's your name?" I asked.

"Krissa."

"Look Krissa, despite that being a good idea." Her eyes lit up. I should not have said that. "It is not safe for you to interfere in this investigation. You should go home and forget you saw or heard anything."

Krissa crossed her arms. "If you don't take me with you, I'll just go by myself."

I ground my teeth. The Provider kept me alive because he thought I may have some value he could use. Slaughtering an innocent civilian to retain confidentiality of the murder wouldn't even raise his heartbeat. Letting Krissa into the investigation risked her life, but letting her intrude on her own asked for her to be killed.

"Fine," I said, residual anger from Valen's appearance turning my tone harder than I wished. "You can come with me to the gate guards, but we are not *interrogating* anyone. We're asking a few simple questions about the safety of visiting Hallow's Promise."

She nodded, wisps of loose hair billowing about her face. "I'll bring my notepad, just in case."

"No, do not bring a notepad. Also, do not go by yourself." I looked over the woman's head, where a line of people waited for their orders. "I need to finish working and have a couple of other tasks to complete. Meet me back here an hour after sunset."

Krissa smiled, a look that etched a hole into my chest. I hoped I wouldn't get her killed.

"I have class this afternoon, but I'll be here. Also, I'll take one of those energy drinks, like you made that one woman. It looked really good."

I clenched my teeth, forced a smile, and got back to work.

***

Even Brew seemed tired by the end of our shift. Its wheels groaned when we returned home, and the door only opened halfway to let us out.

I patted its frame. "You did good. Thank you."

A happy little rumble escaped—its version of a soft laugh.

Bubbles followed me from the wagon. His thick hind legs smacked against the ground like a noisy shadow.

"You know you can leave whenever you want." I gestured toward the surrounding trees.

He stared at me.

"Alright then, let's go."

I didn't go inside. I swore it wasn't because I was afraid. My wards performed perfectly last night, letting me know when intruders had entered. But hesitancy lingered. If the wards warned me again, it wouldn't even matter. I hadn't been able to defend myself. Someone else could have killed me or dragged me back to the capital.

No, I wanted to wait a little longer before going back in there.

A good friend would have checked on Leof. He hadn't asked for more pain relief, so I hoped his recovery went well. But I had barely decided we were friends, much less that I was a good one.

A true friend would have kept their distance in the first place, instead of forming relationships that may put others at risk.

The little cottages turned into larger homes as the cobbled road widened into Hallow's Promise proper. Horses passed by us, riders barely giving a passing glance, and an occasional horse-drawn wagon rattled along. The scent of evergreens faded to musty dung and old ale as several taverns opened their doors for the evening.

People milled through the streets as the workday officially ended. Some chatted with others, haggled over shop prices, and several college students staggered down the streets with bags filled with supplies—or booze. Almost all of them looked at Bubbles with a puzzled, or fearful, expression, but nobody stopped us.

Hallow's Promise didn't offer anything extraordinary, but its arched wooden doors and soft oil lanterns illuminated a sort of comfort I hadn't experienced anywhere else when looking for a place to hide. Anyone could enter these gates and simply become someone else.

The lights ended before Main Street, and we ventured to the edge of the fanfare. A distinct metallic odor oozed from the squat building near the corner. Wind pushed a rickety red sign against the frame, too old and worn to be legible.

I pushed open the door, and the warplog hopped inside, unhindered. In fact, he looked a little brighter-eyed than usual. He probably recognized the smell.

"How can I help you—ah, Rae." The woman at the front counter smiled at me. Matilda's dark hair rolled into a tight bun at the top of her head and an apron protected her simple clothes. Suspicious dark stains marred the white fabric. "I see you brought a . . . pet?"

I smiled at Bubs. "More of a friend, really. I'm here to see if you have something he'd enjoy eating?"

Matilda plucked a rag from her waistband and slid it over the great butcher's blade in her other hand. Rivulets of red liquid stained the towel.

"Warplogs aren't too picky most of the time. As long as it's dead, and the deader the better. They like the bones, too, to carve down their teeth. I think I have some in the back waiting to go out in the garbage tonight. Let me check." She disappeared behind a white sheet into the depths of the butcher shop.

I looked down at Bubs. "Not too picky with food or friends, huh?"

He licked his eyes.

Matilda returned with a long, skinned leg bone. A deep brown with veins of green replaced the usual redness of fresh meat. It didn't smell quite rotten yet, but foul enough that I wouldn't eat it.

Bubbles started drooling.

The shopkeeper laughed and wrapped the leg in sheets of thick paper.

"Warplogs aren't usually fond of people, though this one smells better than the rest. He seems to like you."

"I removed him from a situation potentially dangerous to his health," I said. "Now he won't leave."

She handed the carcass over the counter. I gripped it, surprised at its weight.

"They're a good friend to have, Rae. As long as you keep him well fed."

"Thanks Matilda, I plan to do that." I hesitated. I didn't want to draw more people into this mess, but I was technically supposed to be investigating a murder, and she worked near most of the inns. "You heard about anything odd in Hallow's Promise, have you? Anything about it being unsafe for visitors?"

Her lips split into a crooked smile. "Are you working with Leof again, dear? You said before it would be the last time, and the time before that. Looking at that much death will go to your head, sweetie. You'll be seeing danger in the shadows."

I returned the smile. "Just curious, Matilda."

"I haven't heard anything, dear, but I'll keep an ear out. Most of the travelers avoid my shop anyway. Fresh meat isn't the best travel provision."

"That's true, I guess. Let me know if you do hear anything. How much do I owe you for the meat?"

She waved her hand, thankfully before picking up the giant knife again. "You're doing me a favor by taking it. I'll try to keep some larger chunks that don't sell, for next time. Make sure you keep that precious boy fed, now." She shook her finger at Bubs, who happily thumped his back foot in reply.

"Thanks, Matilda. I'll see you in a couple days."

The bell on the door jingled again as I slipped out and held it until Bubs hopped along. I unrolled my gruesome package and grasped the tip of the bone with two fingers.

"What do you think?" I asked Bubbles.

He studied the meat for a moment. Acid drool leaked, his eyes grew big, and he opened his mouth.

It opened, and opened, stretching impossibly wide, giving me an impressive view of rows and rows of razor teeth. A foul stench of stomach contents oozed around me.

I tossed the meat into the gaping hole. "Ew, you need your teeth brushed."

Bubs snapped his jaws shut. His mouth shrank. It didn't matter that the meat and bone were almost double his body's length. His little round form remained unchanged, and he let out a loud burp.

"Gross," I said, but I felt better knowing he wasn't hungry. "Let's go home. I have a very inconspicuous, not-at-all-an-interrogation to get to."

Chapter 8

I left Bubbles in his cupboard in the wagon. He seemed sleepy after his meal, and happy to curl up on the towel and take another nap.

Eventually, I needed to go inside my house. But not yet.

The intersection near the crime scene didn't take long to reach by foot. The hustle and bustle had settled down, only lingering horse droppings and the impression of wagon wheels remained. Tomorrow, people would pass through again, drawn to the college or Main Street, but tonight, calmness hung in the air.

"Hello!"

At least, it used to.

Krissa straightened from leaning against a tree, and her lips parted to reveal a wide smile. She'd changed into a dark cloak but wore the same brightly colored hair bands around her braids. She smelled good, a simple soap and citrus flavor. It almost tasted like soft orange tea, with the lightest amount of honey to sweeten it.

"Hi," I said as she approached. "You really should change your mind and go home."

Krissa rolled her eyes. "We both know that isn't going to happen. I bet you went through all the possibilities in your head and determined that I'd do my own investigation without you, so it would be safer if we worked together."

I blinked. Could this woman be a mind reader? The power was extremely rare, but not unheard of.

"Let's go," I said. The sooner we talked to the gate guards, the sooner Krissa returned to her safe life.

I expected her to fill the silence as we walked, but she remained quiet, studying the terrain. She seemed to catch every sound the forest offered as her head turned toward even the slightest noise. A light smile broke across her face.

Her gaze made me look, too. Sunset invited cooler air to twine between the trees. A golden shade kissed the green leaves and turned the unpaved road a rich, copper color. Birds chirped, squirrels bickered, and an occasional branch sent an eerie snap through the late fall evening.

The capital had been so different from Hallow's Promise.

"It's so alive here," I mumbled, the surprising contrast catching me unexpectedly.

Krissa turned all that attention to me. "Compared to where?"

"To where I . . . used to live."

"Where was that?"

I pressed my lips. "Far away."

"Near the capital?"

Only luck and sheer will kept me on my feet as the question made me stumble. It took a moment to find my voice. "Why would you ask that?"

She shrugged. "It seems like the capital would be the farthest place from Hallow's Promise."

"Yes, it was . . . near the capital."

"What was it like?"

I knew I should stop talking, that I had told this stranger too much already, but nobody had ever asked me that.

Thoughts lingering in my mind for the five years since I'd left rested on the edge of my tongue, before my better judgment.

"It was louder and darker. Some buildings were taller than the trees, and all were made from dark stone. Even on the brightest days, very little light reached the streets." And the cloaks all Providers wore cast our faces into eternal shadow. "It always smelled good, because horses weren't allowed through the gates and the waste was transported outside the walls. But it was also . . . cold. Less alive. People ducked their heads when they walked by, strangers wouldn't care enough to pause and talk on the streets."

I bit my tongue. I'd told her far, far too much.

"That sounds downright dreary," she said, not looking at me anymore, but back to studying the trees. "I've been to the capital once myself, and it felt rather similar. You must have been very close by indeed."

"Indeed," I echoed, and transitioned to less dangerous questions. "You mentioned you had class this afternoon. What are you studying?"

"Studying? Oh no, I'm an instructor."

My brows rose. I did a double take at her long cotton dress smothered beneath the oversized cape. Her smooth face and petite figure appeared far too young to instruct anyone, much less at the college.

She caught me staring and chuckled. "Don't worry, most people are surprised."

"What do you teach?"

"I teach statistics, the study of how likely an event is to occur via mathematical application. That's why I've been to the capital, actually, to display some statistical data related to previous conflicts compared with our capabilities now. Boring, I know, but I sometimes find numbers easier to understand than people."

"No," I whispered. "That's not boring at all. I completely understand."

I found potions, my wagon, and even a warplog easier to understand than people.

We didn't talk for the last quarter mile, each lost in our own thoughts. The sun slipped below the horizon as we finally reached the gate.

Gray stone walls climbed above the ground. A rusted iron crisscrossing gate set in the center, drawn all the way up, inviting anyone inside. Clusters of guards leaned against the wall and watched with quiet gazes. One tall man fitted in metal armor greeted visitors and inquired about their business in Hallow's Promise.

"What are we going to ask them?" Krissa asked, her eyes wide with an excitement that made my stomach twist.

"*We* are not going to ask them anything. *I* am going to ask if they'd recommend having visitors right now."

Krissy rolled her eyes. "That sounds boring."

"It should be boring. Boring is safe."

"Whatever."

I pressed my lips together and stepped forward. Maybe she was right, and my strategy was boring, but it would get us through this investigation alive and without drawing attention.

The guard sent a couple inside with a light smile. Nobody else waited behind them as the last shadows of the wall faded into the introduction of night.

"Um, hello," I said. My mind suddenly flung all the words from my mouth, and my tongue turned bone dry.

The guard straightened and turned, obviously surprised by someone addressing him from inside the gate. The armor shone as soft torches came alive. Shaggy hair covered a tall forehead, which creased as he eyed me.

"Can I help you?" His hand moved a little closer to the blade on his belt.

I opened my mouth, but all the moisture had fled. My throat felt like dry paper. I choked, which pinched my throat worse, and a horrible cough tumbled from my lips.

Krissa stepped beside me and put a hand on my arm. "She's trying to ask if you could spare a moment of your time? We have some family members considering a visit to Hallow's Promise and would love to hear about the current travel situation."

I reined in the coughing, breathing through my nose until I finally swallowed. The guard looked at both of us, and his brow creased even more.

"You two are related?" The disbelief rang clear. I knew how we looked. My light hair pulled tight in a bun perched at the top of my head. I wore casual breeches and a loose tunic tucked into a leather belt. My boots laced almost to my knees, which protected my legs when I waded through brambles to collect herbs for my potions. Krissa's twisted hair with those vibrant ties looked nothing like me. Her dress peeked beneath the cloak, more fitting for a barmaid than a professor. The tiny shoes clinging to her feet barely functioned as protection.

I looped my arm through hers and gave the guard a wide smile. "Sure are."

He didn't comment again. "Ask, but I can't promise I'll know much. We aren't allowed to leave these walls." A few nearby guards chuckled under their breath.

"Would you, uh, say it's a good time to visit right now?"

"I'd say they should wait for daylight." He smirked.

Anger simmered in my gut. He knew exactly what my question meant and decided to get some entertainment instead.

"She means," Krissa must have sensed my temper, "is this time of year fairly safe to travel to Hallow's Promise?"

"Safe as any, I suppose." He shrugged.

"Is there any reason someone shouldn't travel here right now?" She tried again.

"People can travel whenever they want. If they have the right documentation, we don't give a rat's ass who comes through the gate."

More chuckles followed his words.

I wished I could use my magic. It simmered in warm anger, itching to wrap around the guard and make him answer our questions. I'd always had a leash around my magic. First, the king kept control over it, only allowing me to use it for his benefit. Now, he'd be able to track me if I used too much. I barely even knew what I was capable of.

"Have you heard of anything weird happening? Recently some travelers mentioned refusing to spend the night here. We want to make sure it's safe for our families." Krissa smiled, spilling out more patience than I possessed.

"Look, ladies, the king's policy is simple: if they have papers, they come in. We aren't responsible for personal safety. Is there anything else?"

Krissa's face turned red. I almost saw the sharp words in her mouth. I squeezed her arm.

"No, thank you. We'll be off now." I pulled her away. Starting a confrontation with the guards would not be inconspicuous.

We walked silently for a few moments until the lights from the gate faded away. The woman turned to me, her expression sharp.

"Well, you were right about one thing. That was not an interrogation."

"It's not worth getting arrested for information that likely isn't important. I can't investigate a murder if I'm in prison."

She arched her brow. "You call *that* investigating? You barely said anything!"

The anger returned, more at myself than Krissa. "I don't call that investigating, because I'm not a marshal. I'm a potion maker! I sell tea and tonics from my wagon—I don't solve crimes."

Silver moonlight highlighted streaks in her hair as Krissa crossed her arms. She studied me.

"You must have some kind of experience if that man was threatening you into solving this crime."

I sighed, and the anger melted away. "I know a lot about death. More than one person should, but I don't have any investigative experience. That man's name is Valen, and I'm pretty sure he's going to end up killing me when I fail at solving the murder."

"Kill you? Oh, my—"

"Hey!" A muffled voice escaped from the darkness. I balled my hands into fists as my heart pulsed. Any sort of mischievous person could approach from the shadows. Another reminder of my helplessness. "Wait a moment, please!"

The moonlight brushed over another man in a guard's uniform. He wore a sword on his hip, unsheathed. His chest heaved when he stopped, and he took a moment to catch his breath.

"L-Look," he stuttered, "I wanted to apologize for Blayke's behavior back there. He's an ass." The guard shrugged. "But I know you're concerned about your family, and I wanted to mention something that happened last week."

"What happened?" I asked.

"A couple from the capital were attempting to relocate to Hallow's Promise. They'd left in a rush, from what I understand, something about a business deal gone wrong. It doesn't matter. They arrived at midmorning one day and fled the next night after sundown. They didn't take any of their belongings and only said it wasn't safe for them to stay. I got the sense they'd been threatened, but they wouldn't say any names."

"Did they have a home lined up?" Krissa asked.

The guard shook his head. "No, they had a room at an inn on Main Street. Siren's Sorrow, I believe."

Of course it would be Siren's Sorrow. The dirtiest inn in town accepted any guest, even someone running from the capital. They didn't ask for identification if the coin shone bright enough.

"Thank you for taking the time to tell us." Krissa smiled.

The guard's gaze lingered on her for a moment. His eyes brightened when she returned the expression. "I hope your family isn't planning an extended stay, but I'd reckon a short visit would be safe enough. Have a good night."

He tipped his hat and turned back into the woods.

"That was awfully nice of him," Krissa said. I wondered what he got from the trip through the woods, and if his information was true. Krissa side-eyed me. "That's more investigating than you've done."

I rolled my eyes. "If you want to keep working with me, you'd better shut up."

She smiled, teeth white in the moon's glow. "You want me to keep helping you?"

The truth unveiled right in front of me. I wasn't a marshal. I didn't want to be. But Krissa had passion and a sharp mind, plus an advanced education. It would be unwise to cast her aside.

"It will be dangerous. I'll try my best to keep you out of anything bad, but there may be a time when I won't be able to control it. If you want to accept that risk, then yes, I would love it if you kept helping me."

She grabbed my hand and squeezed. "I'm absolutely in. Find me after class tomorrow evening. We're going to investigate the crap out of this thing."

I squeezed her hand back, and hoped she was right, and that I hadn't signed her death sentence.

***

I leaned my head against the exterior of my door. Bubbles snoozed in my arms. Some point while I'd been gone, he'd regurgitated the leg bone and shredded it to bits all over Brew's floor. I took a few moments to sweep out the shards, which helped me calm down after talking to the guards.

65

"You. Are. So. Stupid," I whispered to myself, lightly hitting my forehead against the wood with each word. "Open. The. Dumb. Door."

Yet my hand wouldn't lift to the knob. My wards remained intact. Nobody had entered my house, but my mind refused to hear the logic. I remembered Valen pressing me against the door and the realization of how helpless I'd become.

"Maybe it'll open if you're nicer to it."

I froze as the familiar voice I'd just been thinking about seeped from the shadows. Valen was exactly the last person I needed right now, in this moment of crisis.

I didn't look up. "Go away."

I felt, rather than saw, him approach. A combination of heat slipping from his body and that earthy scent—like trees and open sky—told me exactly where he stood.

I waited for the next sharpened line, but his voice sounded soft.

"What's wrong?"

The tenderness gathered all the anxiety in my chest and ignited a match. I let the flames eat me from the inside out, the anger, the pain, the fear, until it burned white hot.

I looked up at him. His face flattened, and he leaned back, as though seeing the fire in my gaze and, for a moment, he feared me.

"You are the problem," I whispered. My magic simmered to life, raw, untrained, dangerously close to exposing myself. "I was safe here. I was happy. And you've ruined everything."

Valen raised his lips into a light smile. I saw his death in my mind, and I wondered how it tasted. How that delicious strength and power would flow into me, become mine, what I could do with it.

How I'd have to run, to escape the capital and the king.

"What's wrong with the door?" he asked again. He didn't break his stare from mine. Embers danced in his own eyes, staining the darkness with hints of gold.

He reached out. For a moment, I thought he might touch my face with his fingertips. I tensed, expecting the contact, but oddly anticipating it as well.

His hand moved past me and grabbed the doorknob. The locks tumbled at his touch, despite the lack of a key, and he slipped the door open. The wards chimed in my head, but I let them fade away. My house still smelled like lavender and syrup. It smelled like home.

Valen walked into the dimly lit space. Warmth from the fire spilled through the front door, over to me on the stoop, but it felt somehow cooler than the man who'd just stood there. He walked around the perimeter of my home, fading into the shadows beneath the loft for a moment, then clamored up the stairs in a quick, much-too-graceful motion. A heartbeat later and he jumped down. The dishes on the counter didn't even rattle.

He strode to the door, that half-smile returning.

"Nobody's here."

I stepped inside. The anger had faded. My power died back down. I wanted to sleep.

"Thanks," I said.

Valen reached around me and pressed the door shut. I stumbled, my back hitting the solid wood. He kept one hand on either side of my head, ducking a bit to level his face with mine. My heart jumped. It felt like last night, but not the same. Something else replaced the menace and threats. I didn't want to suck in that sharp scent, so heavy that I tasted evergreen, but I did, until my chest felt like bursting.

Valen leaned his face closer, keeping the rest of his body an arm's length from mine. His breath slipped across my skin and sent goosebumps down my arms.

"Were you happy, Sunshine?"

I opened my mouth, but the man didn't wait for an answer. He swooped beside me and opened the door, controlling his speed enough to prevent me from falling. He disappeared into the woods, taking that intoxicating smell with him.

I drew a shaking breath and stuck my head out the door.

"Go screw yourself!" I yelled into the woods, putting an ounce of power into the words to be sure he heard them. "And my name is Rae!"

His chuckle echoed to me before I slammed the door shut.

Chapter 9

I rarely drank my own potions. Too much exposure risked growing partially immune to their effects. But I made an exception tonight.

The embers inside Brew's oven stoked bright gold, licking the bottom of the cauldron I'd placed in the center. Tiny bubbles simmered at the edges, almost boiling, but not quite.

I'd spent the day at the same intersection near the scene, hoping someone would drop new information. Nothing. At least it'd proven to be a good selling spot, one I'd likely return to, eventually. Or maybe not. Maybe I'd never even go to this side of town once this all ended.

After the later travelers sulked through, I'd closed the shutter, packed up my sign, and Brew took us to the college to wait for Krissa's class to end. Evidently, we arrived early.

Bubbles napped near my feet. A little hiss escaped his tiny nostrils with each exhale, alluding to a calmness I did not feel.

I dug the marble mortar and pestle from the lowest cupboard. One drawer slowly slid open, revealing layers of dark green, dried tea leaves.

"Thanks," I said to the wagon, heaving two hefty spoonfuls of the tea into the mortar. The drawer snapped shut.

Grinding the leaves felt normal, calm, so different from the last two days. My timeline narrowed as each day passed. Eleven days before the Provider returned for their murderer. A murderer I didn't have and didn't know how to find. If I ran before he returned, both Leof and Krissa would be in danger.

The pestle ground hard against the marble, drawing out a terrible screeching sound. I put the bowl on the counter and drew a deep breath. The green tea offered both tranquility and an energy boost–if I finished crafting it.

I poured water into the bowl and exchanged the pestle for a flat-bottom whisk. Tiny bubbles rose and popped as I spun the tool until all the powder incorporated into the liquid. Brew rattled again, and another door opened, revealing rows of prepared syrups. I smiled. The wagon clearly sensed my foul mood and determined I needed to sweeten the night up.

I drew the vanilla syrup from the shelf, dark and thick, the beans suspended inside, and swirled a healthy serving into the tea. After another quick whisk, I poured some into a cup. The sweet and herby scents eased my soul even before the first sip.

Delightful.

Two brisk knocks sounded on the wagon's door. I opened it and ushered Krissa inside. Bubbles cracked one beady eye, gave her a side glance, and went back to sleep. She studied him for a moment, but remained silent.

"Here." I poured a second mug of tea. I had a feeling we'd both need it for tonight.

She smiled and inhaled the smell, then closed her eyes. We leaned on opposite sides of the wagon, not talking, both enjoying our own drinks, and yet . . . I didn't feel lonely at all. The dying fire drove away the evening's chill; Bub's soft snoring and Krissa's cozy smile felt like the most company I'd ever had.

I paused, tea halfway to my lips. It *was* the most company I'd ever had. Sure, I'd been watched constantly in the capital, had worked with Leof and his team, even served long lines of customers for most of my days. Yet, I'd never quietly rested among friends before.

Krissa watched me, those sharp eyes catching everything.

"Want to talk about it?" she asked.

I shook my head. "Nothing to talk about."

"If you say so. What's the plan for tonight's investigation, Madame Marshal?"

"Don't call me that." Krissa smiled wider. "We're going to Siren's Sorrow, talk to the innkeeper there, then leave. Hopefully, they'll be able to tell us something."

She arched her brow. "And if they don't?"

"Then we try something else."

"Great plan, I love it."

"Do you have any better ideas?"

She held both hands up at my tone. "I'm just the trusty assistant, remember? Do you have a horse? How do you plan to get to the Sorrow?" She glanced around, forehead creased. "Actually, I've never seen a horse pull this wagon. How do you move it around?"

Brew vibrated beneath us. Krissa grabbed the cupboard and glanced down. A couple of drawers popped open and shut, Brew's equivalent of a casual snicker.

I froze. The wagon had never revealed itself to anyone else. Doing so risked its destruction and my capture, both of which Brew knew. It either trusted Krissa, or inanimate objects shouldn't be capable of making such risky decisions—partially why so few had ever existed in the first place.

"A magic wagon," she whispered. Her eyes turned distant. "It's been millennia since the sentient objects disappeared, since they hunted the last of their creators to extinction. The probability of a relic being discovered . . ." She looked at me. Pieces of understanding connected across her expression. "It's much more likely a new one was created, which would be impossible without—"

"Don't say it," I whispered. "Words have power."

She nodded, her throat constricting. I snatched her hand and squeezed her fingers. "Don't tell anyone."

"Of course not. They'd kill you. Or worse."

"Much worse."

Her tone brightened. "That explains a lot, actually. Especially how these drinks are so good."

I smiled. "They're just regular drinks, I promise."

"Well, that's boring." She sipped again. "Now, tell me how we're really getting to Siren's Sorrow."

***

Krissa's skin tinted green as she tumbled out of Brew's door. Her knees wobbled, but she remained upright, which made me a little proud.

"I should have warned you that ley line travel can be a bit startling." I wrapped the blanket around Bubbles in his cupboard as Krissa drew deep breaths outside. The warplog licked both of his eyes—which I interpreted as thanks. I followed Krissa out, locking the door behind me.

"'A bit startling,' she says." Krissa turned her voice high pitched, mocking me. "That was downright miserable. I wish I hadn't had that tea now."

"It'll stop in a moment."

"So, this wagon can travel anywhere it wants? In the whole world?"

I shook my head. "No, it can travel along intersecting ley lines, basically rivers of magic that run through the earth. There are wider lines, which travel great expanses, and smaller ones that bleed through most towns and cities. Hallow's Promise has a lot of those small lines, making it convenient to travel almost anywhere. But it can't travel without ley lines."

"Like a magic boat, then." Krissa nodded, still a little green. "Great, that's great. I have a friend with a magic boat. I love that for me."

My heart stuttered as I tried to ignore the casual word 'friend' from her mouth. I was pretty sure she meant *me*.

She stared at me. "Should we go in?"

"Oh, yes, sorry." I needed to clear my mind and refocus on the investigation. Eleven days, eleven days.

Brew had dropped us off on a quiet road a couple of blocks outside of Main Street. We wandered through the stone-structured buildings until turning the corner onto the main road through the center of town. Siren's Sorrow nestled between the darkest of the structures, slightly shorter and quainter than its neighbors.

The inn used to offer shelter and entertainment to visitors of Hallow's Promise. Once the town's population grew, the wall constructed, and a city tax mandated, it quietly became . . . something else. Travelers expected higher class accommodations, turning to the newer inns and taverns. But a new clientele sought after cheaper entertainment, women to warm their beds, and an affordable door with a lock. Thus, Siren's Sorrow filled the gap.

Thick smoke billowed through the front door. Krissa pulled it open and wrinkled her nose at the sharp scent. Few lanterns illuminated the lower tavern portion of the building, and a staircase wound upward from the back corner.

Nobody turned as we stepped inside. People packed wall-to-wall, every table full. I raised a brow. Evidently, the Sorrow's clientele had grown. Women in low-cut peasant tops and tight corsets strode between tables with overflowing platters of food. The simple beef stew and sourdough rolls made my stomach grumble.

One server with curly blonde hair paused and looked us up and down. My loose top and thick pants didn't match the atmosphere of the room, but Krissa's colorful ensemble made up for the disconnect.

The waitress smiled. "Room at the bar, loves." She walked by, forgetting us in a moment to pass along the trays of food to waiting customers.

"I guess we go to the bar," Krissa said. Her wide eyes studied the crowd, like she may be calculating some of those statistics she was so fond of.

"Guess so."

A set of empty chairs rested at the end of the wooded bar top, chipped and dented with years of use. The longer we lingered in the tavern, the more the flavor of pipe smoke built in the back of my mouth. A leather stool cushioned me as we sat, worn and comfortable.

Another waitress appeared. "Two for you?"

I raised a brow.

"Two what?" Krissa asked, before I managed the question myself.

"Two ales, dear. That's all we have for drinks tonight. We've been wrung out of everything else, I'm afraid."

I set a golden coin on the wood. "Two would be great."

She snapped up the coin and disappeared through a side door.

Krissa glanced over her shoulder. "I didn't expect it to be so crowded."

The waitress returned and smashed two overfull mugs in front of us. She gave Krissa a wink when she passed hers over, and the professor blushed.

"Excuse me, can I ask a question?" I said before she hurried to the next customer. The waitress paused and smiled, lingering for a moment.

"Call me Lillie, dear, and I'll answer any question you two lovely ladies have." Another glance to Krissa, who studied the bar silently.

"I'm new to town—just arrived today." I smiled, wishing the lie felt better in my mouth. "Are the inns here always so busy?"

Lillie shook her head. "Not usually. There's the Barley Festival this weekend though, right outside of town. It's got all the inns booked up, and we've caught the overflow. Can't say we're upset about it. Probably fill the coin banks till next year. You must not be here for the festival?"

I shook my head. "No, I'm actually planning to move to Hallow's Promise. I have friends that live here," I nudged Krissa with my elbow, "and they seem to like the place."

"Ah, a local, then." She smiled at Krissa. "Most folk find Hallow's Promise suits their needs. Some stay a while and move along. You'll find out which you prefer rather quickly. I'll have to be off for a moment. I have some orders ready."

We waited for Lillie to dart back into the kitchen, and I lowered my voice to a whisper.

"Nothing seems suspicious to me," I said.

Krissa glanced around. "Everyone's in a good mood. I do wish they'd put out the pipes."

A golden fire warmed the large room thoroughly. Laughter, food, and drinks abounded. The Sorrow didn't offer anything overtly formal, but it had a pleasant feeling. I sipped my ale; the light flavor wasn't the best, but was certainly adequate.

"I'm going to wander through the room and see if anything stands out," Krissa said.

I smiled and nodded. I doubted anything relevant to the case would be in plain sight, but I also needed Krissa away to speak to the waitress privately for a moment. Involving my new friend in the investigation was risky enough. I didn't need her putting her life in danger with me.

Lillie came back, and her smile faded a bit as she tracked Krissa on the other side of the room.

"Can I get you anything else, dear?" she asked me half-heartedly.

"I'm hoping I can book a room here. I got a few questions first, though."

She smiled. "Sure, dear, ask anything."

"Would you say it's a safe place to stay? As a single woman traveler, I can't be too careful."

Lillie shrugged. "It's as safe as any inn, I suppose. We haven't had much trouble. If you're in the room before the witching hour, it'll probably be quiet."

I arched a brow. "Probably?"

She winked. "The Siren's Sorrow is what it is, dear. Not a lot of ruckus this week, but last week was another story."

"What happened last week?"

"One couple paid for a week's stay and left after the first night. Claimed someone attacked them in their room, but we didn't see any damage. I think they wanted a refund, but the owner refused to return their coin. They left anyway, abandoning heaps of stuff the staff had to sort through." Lillie rolled her eyes.

"That seems odd." I tapped my fingers along the bar.

"Not really, dear. Customers say lots of things to get their coins back. It was just another day in the hospitality business. Now, can I book you a room?"

I smiled and hoped she didn't see the suspicion in my eyes. "Yes, for tomorrow, please. I have accommodations with my friend for tonight."

Lillie drew out a thick, leather-bound record book from beneath the bar. She flipped through the pages and dipped a feathered pen into a small ink bottle.

"Name, dear?"

"Rae," I said. She didn't ask for a last name.

"It'll be one coin to hold the room." I passed the fee along. She stuffed it inside a satchel and tied the top. "Where did you say you were moving from?"

"The capital," I said, making my voice strong, but casual. I'd never admitted the words before, and they felt wrong—far too close to the truth and my secrets. "I'm ready for a big change. Would the room be on the ground floor?"

"The second floor. The ground floor is reserved for a different type of guest." The waitresses' eyes shined as she shoved the satchel and book beneath the counter and walked away.

Krissa reappeared.

"Anything helpful?"

She shook her head. "I may have a chance at a second career if I want to delve into some . . . extracurricular activities, but nothing else. You?"

I returned the gesture. If I told Krissa about the room I'd booked for tomorrow and how I set up my information to mirror that of the couple that had been threatened, she'd insist on staying with me. I refused to risk her life that way.

"I want to look outside for a minute." I stood from the stool and paused. "Do you want to say goodbye to the server first?"

Krissa straightened, avoiding eye contact. "Why would I do that?"

"Just thought I'd ask." I shouldered around her. We navigated between masses of people to the door. The thick wooden slab slid open soundlessly and closed before any rowdiness escaped into the night. Main Street settled, cool and calm.

I wrapped around the side of the building. Krissa glanced over her shoulder, then followed. We crouched in the shadows and ducked beneath the soft glows slipping through the windows.

"What are we doing?"

"Lillie said the rooms for the inn are on the second floor. We don't have any witnesses to whatever happened to the couple from the capital, but someone threatened them. I'm assuming it occurred here, at the inn."

Rows of windows stacked neatly on top of each other. The lower ones filled mostly with shadows illuminated by the tavern fire, but a few were jarringly darker. Occasional low noises and soft chuckles floated through the thin panes. I didn't linger to hear more.

We skirted the edge of the building. Everything appeared orderly, cleaner than I expected.

"The rumors for travelers to avoid Hallow's Promise seems to be poorly spread," Krissa whispered.

My brow creased as I studied the wall along the east side, tucked between the neighboring building. A thin line of loose dirt ran along that side and spread into a wide flower bed beside the western wall. The stones climbed in an offset pattern up the building. Darkness in the mortar lines showed the seams of the construction. Something appeared out of place, but I couldn't quite figure out what.

"The inn is packed. You'd expect a lot more murders if the killer was targeting visitors to the area."

I turned to her. "Say that again."

"It seems the killer would have his choice of victims if he hated travelers so much."

"That's a good point." An excellent point, one I should have realized right away. The killer hadn't targeted any random visitor, he targeted people from the capital. First, the couple had been terrorized into leaving, then the Provider had been killed.

One large shadow moved from the tavern window, casting more light. The thick lines of mortar clarified.

Rough cracks cut into the seams of the eastern wall, almost hidden in the gaps between stone blocks. They didn't blend into the mortar quite enough to be invisible, though only someone paying attention would notice anything at all.

I stepped closer and paused, an outlined impression in the dirt catching my attention. I bent down for a closer look.

A paw print. Too large to be a regular canine.

A werewolf.

My heart sank. I leaned into the wall, bracing myself with two hands, and studied the cracks along the mortar. The sharp, rough gouges could easily be werewolf claws piercing between the stones. I tracked them up to a second-story window, where dirt smudged on the exterior appeared like fog in the shadows.

"What do you see?" Krissa asked.

No use hiding this information. I stepped back and let her see the impression.

"A paw print? Like a dog?"

"Or a wolf," I said.

Her eyes widened. "A werewolf? Do you think this is a clue?"

I pressed my lips together but didn't answer. I feared it may be a clue, the most important one I'd discovered yet. But I wanted to be wrong. The only wolf possibly involved in this case, I had recently decided, was my friend.

I forced a smile and turned away. "I think that's enough for today. I need to talk to Lillie one more time, then we can go."

Chapter 10

A knock on the door woke me up. I should have been up already and at the college with Brew, but I didn't have enough energy. If I intended to complete this investigation, I needed more sleep.

And another sunrise meant another day gone before the Provider returned. Ten more days.

Bubbles grunted with displeasure at the disturbance. He'd regurgitated more of the bone from Matilda and snuggled one long sliver in his bed. It bore thick lines where his razor teeth etched into its surface.

My wards buzzed lightly as another knock sounded. I threw a thick cloak over my bed clothes and hurried down the ladder. The flames in the fire perked up as I passed, heating a kettle of water I'd placed on the stand the night before. Fresh herbs waiting to be picked overflowed from pots in the windowsills. I'd need to make more syrups soon.

I blinked at the sunlight invading the house as I drew the door open.

It took me a moment to recognize the man in the doorway. Constable Gerrin smiled down at me. The sun tinted his hair a warm amber color, and he wore a brighter expression than I'd seen on the night of the murder. He looked far too happy for the morning hour.

I forced a smile. "Constable, how can I help you?"

"Marshal Leof is requesting your presence at the morgue. He says it's something only you can help with, ma'am."

At least Leof must be recovering well if he'd resumed the investigation, too. A flicker of relief sparked inside me, cut by a sudden sharp edge of suspicion. Why had there been werewolf tracks at the Siren's Sorrow?

"Did he say what for?"

"No, ma'am."

A little thud escaped from behind me. Small, rhythmic thumps followed, and Bubbles appeared at my ankles. He stared up at the constable, a rather blank look on his flat face.

Gerrin grimaced. "You still have this . . . creature?"

I looked down at the warplog. "He won't leave. I've tried to let him go several times."

"Too bad. Let me know if you ever need help getting rid of it."

"I don't think I'll need any help. You can let Leof know I'll be at the morgue in an hour."

The constable glanced around my property. "Will you need a ride?" He gestured to the handsome stallion tied near the road.

"No, thanks. I'll manage."

Gerrin's brow creased, but he didn't ask anything else. "Perhaps I'll see you there."

I smiled, nodded, and closed the door. My wards pulsed for a moment, then settled as the constable stepped down from the porch and off my land.

An hour—just enough time for a strong, sweet cup of green tea.

***

The morgue resembled little more than a glorified shack, lined with tall, slender windows. Leof saw me walking down the street and propped the door open. Even if he were involved in driving away the couple from the capital, I was relieved that he'd healed.

"You look . . . better," I said.

"Always the best compliments."

"I try." Stepping around the wolf, I paused in the doorway. I'd walked through many doors with Leof at my back, but this felt different. It almost didn't happen. He could have died. The only reason I suspected his involvement in the crime was because of some coincidently placed paw prints. It didn't seem like enough yet.

I turned and put my hand on his arm. "I'm glad you're okay."

His brow creased. "Is something wrong with you?"

"I'm trying to be serious."

"Well, stop. It's weird for you."

I rolled my eyes. "Just shut up and show me the dead guy."

"That sounds more like you."

A staircase to the right of the entryway descended into darkness. Coolness leaked from the shadows, layered with the light sweetness of decay. Leof led the way, and I followed.

The staircase opened into a wide room deep below the ground. The brightness always surprised me. Rows of carefully placed mirrors lined the ceiling and walls, directing sunlight from the upper level to illuminate the underground cavern perfectly. Wooden shelves sat along the natural stone walls, each bearing a body covered with a dark sheet. The depth of the facility provided a natural coolness, but the college also sent students to set cooling spells every few months.

The Provider from the crime scene lay nude on the table. Redness soaked into his legs where the most blood had pooled after death. His glassy eyes appeared even more vacant now. The rope previously entangled around his neck spread across the wooden table beside him.

"Look at this." Leof beckoned me to the other side of the table.

The circular wound I'd seen before appeared clearer now. Three tight letters sat in the center of the mark: CRG.

"Initials?" I asked.

"That would be my best guess, unless it's an acronym of some kind."

Names long ago lost their sentimental meaning and reverted into a population management system for Erline—the capital. The mother's surname replaced the center name, and the father's became the permanent surname. This allowed the capital to trace families with rebellious histories, in case treason ran in the blood. 'R' would represent the mother's lineage, and 'G,' the father's.

I leaned closer to the wound. The initials were lighter than the circle surrounding them. They were set deeper into whatever tool created the mark than the exterior.

"Did you scent map this already?" I asked before moving too close and risking covering the perpetrator's scent with my own.

"I did." Leof sounded less than pleased. "Not a scent on it at all."

"Wolfsbane." I didn't need to see Leof to know he nodded. The herb neutralized a werewolf's ability to separate individual scents. "Whoever did this knew a werewolf would be involved in the investigation."

"It's common these days, but they seemed to have some kind of privileged information. Ah, here's Alivia. She can explain her findings."

The mortician appeared through an open archway on the opposite side of the room. She wore a stiff, black cloak that trailed almost to the ground. Thick gloves lined both arms, up to her elbows, and a tight mask pressed against her face, with a slot to replace the air-cleansing herbs in the front of the garment. Her white hair was a stark contrast to her clothing, pulled up in a tight bun.

"Rae, it's always a pleasure to see you." She didn't offer a hand, and neither did I. I knew what those dark gloves had touched.

"Likewise, Alivia." I forced a smile. The mortician and I had a rocky start, but I liked to think we'd found some common ground after I'd helped her nephew recover from a nasty bout of Thick-Lung with some of my potions.

"Can you fill Rae in on what you just told me?"

Alivia glided over, or at least appeared to. She leaned across the body, the scent of mint and rosemary escaping from her mask.

"I began the examination at the ligature. In a classic suicide by strangulation, I'd expect to see bruising around the rope. Yet you can see this man's skin is evenly toned where the noose was cut." She rolled the body onto his side. "And here, along the spine, you can feel the broken vertebrae below the skull."

Alivia grabbed my hand before I could pull it away. Her silken touch guided my fingers to the cold skin, slipping them over his bones until one felt considerably looser than the rest.

"There," she said. "What is peculiar about that one?"

I studied the bloodless impression where the ropes had been. "The break is too high. The noose would have broken the neck much lower, if at all."

"Very good," she said. I snatched my hand back, and Alivia continued without hesitation. "The marshal stated you noticed the knot on the left side at the scene. Very astute observation." She placed the man on his back again and picked up his right hand. "This hand contains many callouses, common for one with his employment." Most Providers were skilled in hand-to-hand or weaponry combat. "The other does not. I expect this to be his dominant hand."

"He wouldn't have tied the noose to the left, then."

"It would have been difficult and unexpected."

I pressed my lips. The man's neck had been snapped before he'd been strung up on the rope, and the killer had used wolfsbane to cover his tracks. Leof's gut had been right. This was definitely a murder.

"Is there anything else?" I asked.

"I will perform the internal examination and report any unusual findings to the marshal." Alivia glanced up from the body. "Unless you'd like to stay and observe?"

It took all my self-control to avoid making a face.

"No, thanks. Leof can tell me what you find."

She gave a half bow. "As you wish."

I retreated to the wash bin near the staircase and rubbed harsh lye soap into my skin. The slight burn reassured me.

"What do you think made that mark?" Leof asked.

I shrugged. "Could be anything. A tool, a branding iron. The circular shape is unique."

"It's too small for most tools or irons. It has a . . . delicate appearance."

He was right. The flow and shape of the letters inside the circle appeared elegant, ornamental.

"I'll keep thinking about it. Say, did you keep the tipped glass that had been on the table?"

Leof's brow creased. "Of course I did. Why?"

"Did you scent map that, too?"

"Yes, it didn't have anything either."

"Great. I mean, not great, but can I borrow it? I want to test a theory."

"Are you going to tell me that theory?"

"I will if it's right."

The wolf studied me with dark eyes. A hint of a smile appeared, and he shook his head. "You know I'll give you anything if you say it might help a case, Rae."

"*Might*," I said.

"The glass is at the station. I'll bring it over tonight."

"Tomorrow. I have plans tonight."

Leof chuckled. "Something more important going on beside the capital breathing down your neck?"

I smiled. If he was involved in scaring off that couple—or possibly the murder—I certainly couldn't tell him about my plans for the night.

"Something like that," I answered instead.

Chapter 11

Bubbles didn't notice as I slipped out the door later that night. He'd swallowed another leg I'd picked up on my way home from the morgue and digested it in his sleep. When I got home tomorrow morning, there'd probably be bone shards all over the floor.

His peaceful snores followed me through the door. I smiled. It was worth sweeping up a few shards to keep him around.

Brew took me to the same side road as the night before. I patted the wagon's frame.

"Go home for the night," I said. "Come back in the morning."

A few creaks confirmed that the wagon heard my request, though whether Brew listened to me depended on its mood. I drew my cloak tighter and slipped into the shadows of the street.

Siren's Sorrow appeared even more full than yesterday. Dark shapes filled the windows, flashes of firelight escaping as people milled about inside. A noise-reduction enchantment must cover the building, as not a single sound escaped.

I circled the corner, meandering to the east side where the paw prints and sharp lines in the mortar had been. They remained the same. The tracks had faded a bit, worn with the passing of another day, but the rough gouge impressions in the stone wall lingered.

"What are you looking at?"

I jumped and whirled. Valen stepped from the shadows, his arms crossed, a smug smile on his lips. My heart pounded as a sharp annoyance bit in my chest. He moved so quietly and always showed up at the most inconvenient times.

"It doesn't matter to you." I spun on my heels to put my back on him. Immediately, goosebumps rose on my arms and a shiver cascaded down my spine. All my senses fixed on the man, and I wished I'd faced him instead.

That earthy heat brushed across my back. His steps were silent, but I felt every inch as he drew closer, tinted with an invisible presence.

"Everything you do matters to me." Wisps of his breath touched the back of my neck. I refused to flinch, to show him he rattled me at all. "After all, I'm getting paid to babysit you."

I straightened. Of course, the mercenary was only here to ensure I didn't flee town before solving the murder. He'd leave once I found the killer. Good, the sooner the better.

"I am not a baby," was my only reply, and it barely earned a chuckle from the man.

He moved beside me, following my gaze. I shifted to watch his face. His eyes sharpened, tracking every detail along the ground and building. He lingered at the tracks, at the markings on the stone, then moved higher where I knew curious smudges clouded the upper window.

He looked down at me. All that intelligence deliberately slipped away, and one side of his mouth tilted up. The intensity of his gaze dulled.

"So, what are you looking at?" he asked.

I narrowed my eyes. He'd seen the same marks as me, had reached the same conclusions, I was sure of it. But he didn't want me to know. Or he wanted to test my capacity to solve a murder, which I'd already admitted was slim.

I started deep into his gaze, and his eyes widened to my satisfaction.

"An idiot," I said, and turned toward the door.

Valen remained quiet for a moment, something heavy brewing at my back, then a slight laugh followed me.

"Always a pleasure, Sunshine."

I reached the heavy door to the Sorrow. The man waited behind me.

"You're going inside?" I asked, unsure of what I wanted his answer to be.

"I'm already here. Ought to enjoy a drink with the lovely company I've found tonight."

I ground my teeth but pulled open the door.

Noise assaulted us. Laughter, raised voices, the beats of sultry music in the background. Servers clad in aprons and long skirts or pants darted between the thick crowd. Trays of fresh bread and ale balanced on their palms and the weaving dance required to navigate the room didn't rock a single step.

Valen passed me and headed to the bar. I trailed him. The sheer number of people would make it difficult to find any additional clues in the tavern. I hoped the room I'd rented and the tales I'd woven offered enough for the potential murder to investigate me.

A different server managed the bar. His long hair pulled back to display a sharp chin and thin lips.

"Ales?" he asked, not even looking at us.

"Two," Valen said, and I didn't correct him. I hadn't planned to drink during tonight's investigation, but it may be required if the man insisted on staying for any amount of time.

"Why so full?" the mercenary asked when the server returned with two overflowing mugs.

"Barley Festival tomorrow," the man's clipped voice answered before he moved over to the next customer.

I guzzled half the ale. The brew warmed the bottom of my stomach.

"Do you have a plan for the investigation, or is this just a regular facility you frequent?"

"I have a plan," I snapped, wondering about the truth of the words. I opened my mouth again, armed with an insult, but it faded.

Damn, the man looked amazing. The warm, flickering fire turned his skin and hair golden. His blue eyes flickered with light humor as those full lips gave me another smug smile. He wore a white tunic and black breeches, long sleeves exposing large hands which seemed to have a gentle, but firm, grip on the wide mug. He kept my gaze as he lifted the ale to his lips and sipped the liquid as amber as his face.

I blinked. The familiar flames of hate uncurdled inside me. The mercenary had no right to threaten me, follow me, then look this good.

"I have a plan," I said again. "And it doesn't involve you."

"Everything you do involves me. For ten more days, at least."

I rolled my eyes, though the mention of my deadline made my heart skip a beat.

I scanned the crowd. Most looked the way I imagined someone attending a Barley Festival would look. Casual cotton tunics and dresses, with simple slippers or work boots. Most people laughed easily, ale foam on their upper lips. The Sorrow may not offer the finest facilities, but it had a casual and warm atmosphere.

One man near the fireplace did a cursory scan of the room. Tall, thin-faced with dark skin. He caught my eye, and I gave him a flirty smile and dropped my gaze to my ale. When I half glanced up, the stranger was navigating the crowd toward me.

"What are you doing?" Valen whispered harshly.

"Investigating," I answered.

"Hello," the stranger's deep voice said from in front of me. I looked up and caught his eye, smiling wider and tilting my head.

"Hi."

"Might I ask what this beautiful lady's name is?"

I blinked lightly. Being addressed in the third person felt strange, but I let it roll off me.

Valen kept his back to us, but his spine was straight. That darker emotion I'd felt outside simmered again, thick and potent. Anger, probably, or annoyance.

"You can call me Sunshine," I said.

The mercenary jerked his head toward me, a glare on his face. The thickness intensified, brushing across my skin almost tangibly. Definitely anger, cold and dangerous. Nobody else turned our way. Only I felt all that emotion centered on me.

I winked. He turned back, the anger fading. I'd rattled him this time, and he knew it.

"Sunshine," the stranger said. I returned my attention to him. "Such a fitting name for a bright, young woman."

"What's your name?"

"My friends call me Asad." A slight accent softened his vowels.

"Where are you from, Asad?" I took another sip of my ale, tracking his gaze along my lips. Perfect. Enough interest to keep him answering my questions, but not enough to invite unwanted advances.

"My friends and I are from Mistide, by the sea near the east."

Mistide was a small coastal village, known for their bustling seafood trade and thick fog that rolled in with the tides, almost enveloping visibility completely. Their captains learned the tides and coastlines to avoid crashing in the mist.

"Are you here for the festival tomorrow?"

Asad nodded. "One can only have so many fish before celebrating any other variety of food. Will your Sunshine be brightening the festivities as well?"

"Unfortunately, not. I've just left the capital and am planning to call Hallow's Promise home for a while."

He raised a brow. From my periphery, I caught Valen glance at me as well.

"One must experience quite a change from the capital."

"I wanted a change like that." The first true thing I've said tonight.

"Please, I'd love to introduce you to my friends." Asad put his hand on the small of my back. I forced a smile and let him guide me from the bar. Enticing the potential murderer to target me meant spreading my faux story around as much as possible. Talking to the patrons would be the only way to do that.

Asad led me into the crowd. The overwhelming noise and chatter consumed me, sweat mixed with the smell of fire.

I glanced back once. Valen watched me slip away until the press of people swallowed my view.

***

A few hours among the crowd didn't reveal any new clues, but I figured the rumors of my relocation to Hallow's Promise spread well enough. I'd spent a decent amount of time with Asad and his friends, then mingled with a few other larger groups. The ale and food made everyone talkative, and I almost wanted to attend the Barley Festival tomorrow.

The crowd thinned as people peeled off to bed. When only a spattering of folks remained, I said goodnight to the woman I was talking to and ventured back to the bar.

Valen remained in the same spot. He watched me approach, not a word on his lips.

Lillie paused behind the bar and greeted me with a smile.

"Hello again, dear. Are you ready for your room? I see you've made quite a few friends tonight. Too bad so many are visiting, or you'd be well connected in your new home by now." She pulled out the same page as yesterday and tracked the quill through my name.

"Yes, it's too bad."

Lillie tugged a brass key from her pocket, with room number 201A engraved on its front. A thick chain wrapped through a hole in the key, so it wouldn't be easily lost.

"There you go, dear. Third room on the east side, as you requested yesterday. Not sure why you want that specific one, though. I promise they're all the same."

Valen moved closer. "The east side?"

"Thank you, Lillie." I ignored the mercenary. "I glimpsed the room through the window last night and knew it would be perfect."

"I'll talk about checking out in a moment. Let me take these dishes to the back." Lillie disappeared around the bar.

Valen's scent strengthened, and I felt him near my arm. "You're staying the night in that room."

I turned toward him. "What room?"

"And you've been telling everyone you're from the capital all night."

"It's none of your business where I'm from or what I tell people."

He grabbed my arm and turned me to face him. His grip on my skin felt like ice and fire at the same time. The hard lines of his chest were so close to mine that a deep breath would make us touch.

I breathed shallowly.

"You can't stay in that room," he said.

I jerked my arm away. His hand lingered in the air for a moment, then he slowly lowered it.

"You and your *employer* told me to do whatever it takes to solve this murder. You threatened me, my friends, and my livelihood. I have a self-proclaimed babysitter now. You do not get to control how I handle this investigation unless you plan to eliminate yourself as a threat against me."

Valen watched me, that tint of thick anger pooling again.

"I'm staying with you."

I froze. "Absolutely not."

He looked over my shoulder toward the door. "Ask for an adjacent room, then. I need to grab a few things, but I am staying."

The man shouldered past me. Darkness and cold whirled inside before he slammed the door, rattling the hinges.

Lillie sent a disapproving look his way while she returned. "Sorry for the interruption, dear. Check out is at the midday meal, but you're welcome to pay for another night then, if you want to stay. No need to decide right now. We don't offer breakfast, but the bakery at the corner is quite good and opens at sunrise."

"Thanks Lillie." I took more coins from my breeches. "I'd also like another room. I have a new . . . acquaintance unexpectedly looking for a place to stay."

"We're booked up tonight, I'm afraid. Tomorrow ought to be wide open, but the place is packed with the festival tomorrow. Your room was the last we filled yesterday."

I clenched my fist. "There are no more rooms?" Surely, I had heard her wrong.

She shook her head. "'Fraid not, dear. Sorry, I've got to be off now. I hear the cook calling from the kitchen. Will you need anything else while I'm back there?"

"Yes, another ale please."

I dropped my head in my hands and sucked in deep breaths. Valen would happily accept the room and I could go home, but I didn't trust the man with my investigation. Plus, he'd report everything to the Provider, and I wanted to manage that narrative as much as possible.

No, I had to stay at the Sorrow tonight. And Valen would stay with me.

And we only had one room.

Chapter 12

"Cozy." Valen surveyed the room with those sharp eyes, taking in every detail.

It didn't take long. One bed sat in the center, cushioned by squat tables on both sides. A worn armchair rested near the window, stained with so many colors, it made me afraid to look closely. The hardwood floor bore scratches and scrapes, and more than one large circular dent. One door on the west wall revealed a tiny washroom, with a commode and a wash bin. Two towels shared a hook.

Cozy wasn't the right word. *Modest* would be too generous. *Sad* captured the tone best.

I stepped past Valen and hesitated. I wanted to lock the door but didn't want to be trapped inside with him, either.

The mercenary gave me a half-smile and turned the deadbolt. I remained quiet.

I lifted my bag onto the bed, deliberately ignoring that it was the only one in the room. Glass and silver clanked from my satchel. I claimed one side table and layered cups, simple reed candles, and a wooden box onto the small, flat surface.

"What are you doing?" Valen asked.

"Investigating."

I lit one end of a reed, letting its pinpoint light grow into a flame before slipping it to the window. Valen followed a few steps behind me—a quiet, concerning shadow at my back.

The window split into four glass panels, about the width of my hand. Thin, wooden borders sectioned off each panel. I carefully allowed the candlelight to shine against the glass at a slight angle. The smaller point of illumination focused on the glass more thoroughly than a large fire would have.

The top two panes appeared clear, but the smudges I'd seen outside sharpened on the bottom right panel. The rough shape of fingers pressed near the top, where I'd expect someone to push against to open the window. An unbidden smile creased my lips.

"You've found something." Valen saw everything.

"Maybe."

I exchanged the candle for one of the small, round cups. I severed a section of cotton cloth, dropped it into the bottom of the cup, and dipped the candle inside to set the fabric aflame.

I didn't look at Valen, but I imagined his surprise.

A thin, sharpened blade remained at the bottom of my bag. I pulled it out and pressed it against the very edge of the glass windowpane, careful at the top to avoid distorting the external smudges.

"What can I do?" Valen asked. I tensed, my blade almost slipping. I'd expected, perhaps even invited, sarcastic or demeaning questions. His offer of assistance left me unprepared.

"Watch."

I finished scoring the windowpane, then returned to the cup. The cotton extinguished with a simple breath and a sharp burst of light smoke. Heat from the glass soaked into my palm, not too hot.

I pressed the warm cup against the bottom corner of the panel, well away from the smears I wanted to preserve. My hand didn't shake or waver as the cup slowly cooled against my skin. I gave it a light wiggle. No hint of movement shook the jar.

Perfect.

I deepened the score on the window with the blade, carefully pulling the panel toward me as it adhered to the cup. Once the last corner of the windowpane succumbed to my blade, I pulled the entire piece inside, trapped tightly against the suction of the cup, and led it toward the wooden box waiting on the table.

"How did you do that?" Valen's voice sounded cautious. "I didn't sense any magic."

"The world doesn't require magic to do great things." I slipped prongs over the edges to secure the glass, except at the top. "It only requires some hard thinking, and lots of determination."

I closed the box and latched the tiny mechanism to lock the lid. When I turned, Valen's head tilted, and he looked at me with a narrow gaze.

"Who are you, Sunshine?" he asked, his voice low.

"I'm Rae."

A thin layer of animal horn, harvested only after a humane death and all the meat had been distributed for food, rested on the table. I opened a small jar and extracted a thick brush. The white substance from the jar formed a thick paste, and I applied it to the window, where I'd recently freed the glass pane. When a proper amount attempted to ooze down the edges, I slipped the horn shard inside and waited for the substance to dry.

"What's that?"

"It's a sticky paste, made from boiling down fish bladders. Once it dries, it creates a strong binding, so the horn will remain where the severed panel used to be."

Valen crossed his arms. "And why are you doing it?"

I sent him a glare. "I don't want to be cold all night."

His chuckle warmed me more than I cared to admit. "I can keep you warm all night, Sunshine."

I bit my tongue, glad my back remained to him as my cheeks heated.

When the paste dried enough, I released my grip on the horn sheet. It held in place. I let out a sigh of relief and spun around.

The room was empty.

I paused for a moment, but the flash of candlelight beneath the washroom door said Valen was inside. Good. I welcomed a moment alone.

Once I packed my supplies and the box containing the pane, I faced the single bed with my hands on my hips. I refused to share a bed with that man. Few options remained, mostly which part of the floor did I want to sleep on?

I sighed and dragged a pillow and the comforter from the top of the bed. Attempting to convince Valen to sleep on the floor was a level I refused to stoop to. I could sleep there myself, and had slept in far worse places, though not for quite a long time.

The reed candle extinguished as I settled into my makeshift bed. I placed my back to the mattress, not particularly wanting to study what the Siren's Sorrow harbored beneath its bedframes.

Golden light overwhelmed the room, then darkened as the washroom door closed. Valen's steps echoed, then paused.

My heartbeat filled my ears as I waited for the man to break the silence. I hoped he thought I was asleep already, doubtful as that seemed.

The smack of something malleable falling to the ground rose from the other side of the room. Rustling soon followed, then a spattering of creaks as the floor protested from the motion.

I tried to quell my curiosity, but it was the sounds I didn't hear—the cracking and shifting of the wooden bedframe—that made me roll over and peer beneath the bed legs to the other side of the room.

Valen stared back at me, cushioned by a thick pile of sheets, one white blanket pulled up to his stomach, and laughter lit his blue eyes.

But I couldn't find the air to be annoyed. The mercenary had shed his tunic, revealing those promised sculpted lines across his chest and torso, and winding thick rows of muscles down his arms. Even his neck looked wider, propped on one hand so he could see me better through the underside of the bed.

His brows raised. "What are you looking at?"

Chapter 13

I choked and turned away quickly. Too quickly. He laughed from the other side of the bed frame.

My mind went blank.

"Why?" The word slipped out, and I coughed. I didn't have a follow-up question. Why did he take his shirt off? Why did he have to be such a bad person, but look so, so good? Why did he represent everything I hated—everything I'd tried so hard to avoid?

Why did he call me Sunshine?

"Why aren't you on the bed?" I finally fumbled for coherent words.

"It didn't seem right to let a lady slept on the ground."

I snorted. "You don't think I'm a *lady*."

"Hm, I guess that wouldn't be my first choice to describe you." I stared at the ceiling, refusing to let the words hurt me. But Valen kept going, "Maybe determined, or persistent, or overly confident, but probably not a lady."

Why did those words warm my chest?

"Surely you have a better way to describe me now, besides 'idiot.'" His tone sounded light, but genuine curiosity lingered beneath.

Attractive, annoying, intruding . . .

"Honest." My voice surprised me.

I turned to look at Valen, where he still watched me. He didn't wipe the shocked expression away fast enough to hide it from me.

"Why would you say that?" he whispered.

"It's true," I said. "You've threatened me, followed me, interfered in my investigation, but you've never lied to me."

He let the silence overwhelm us for a few moments. Then his face split into a bright smile again, and I rolled my eyes at the upcoming sarcasm.

"So, where are you really from, Sunshine? You know far too much to be raised in this little town your whole life."

I studied the shadows on the walls. I guess talking while we waited to see if someone might threaten or attack us was better than nothing.

"Far away from here."

"How did you end up selling drinks from a wagon?"

I released a reluctant chuckle. "When I . . . got here, I only had Brew and my knowledge of potions. I sold a potion to an overworked professor at the university who couldn't sleep. Then, he tracked me down the next day, and the next. I realized I could use my knowledge of herbs and magic to help people, really help them. I set Brew up with everything I needed to serve drinks, and the rest fell into place."

"Where did you learn all of that?"

I shrugged. "I wasn't allowed to learn many things as a child. I made it a mission to learn as much as possible. Libraries became my second home."

"What's the deal with the werewolf marshal?"

I pressed my lips together. Even if the Provider had been the one hurting Leof, Valen had been involved. "Leof found me sleeping in the wagon right after I started selling my potions. He gave me a room in his house, and a semi-stable income until I got myself back on my feet."

"Semi-stable?"

I half shrugged. "He recognized my experience with death and chaos pretty quickly. He dragged me to investigate his crime scenes and paid more than I was worth."

"Unlikely."

"Once my sales with Brew stabilized, he sold me the house where I live. It used to be family property, but it's just him and Suzie now. He gave me a good price and stopped calling me for every investigation."

"Only the murders," Valen said.

"Only the murders," I echoed. "How about you? How did you end up as a mercenary for a Provider you clearly dislike?"

"Clearly?" He snorted. "I thought my acting skills were impeccable."

"Answer the question."

His blue eyes darkened and he looked at the floor, the wall, anything except my face. "I found myself somewhere I never expected, never wanted, to be. When I end up being the light in a room, you know the rest of the world has gone piss dark."

"That's not a real answer."

He smiled, catching my eyes again. "Yes, it is. Someday, you'll understand."

"Someday? You'll sprint out of Hallow's Promise as soon as the Provider hands you the payload."

"*Sprint* is a strong word. Maybe *hurry* or *walk quickly*."

I rolled my eyes again. They'd start hurting if I kept it up. "What does a mercenary do when you're not threatening women for money?"

"The usual—pillaging, plundering, generally laying waste to the land."

My laughter filled the room again. I didn't want to give him the satisfaction of knowing that I enjoyed the conversation, but the week had offered so few moments of laughter that I couldn't hold it in.

I realized that I didn't want to.

We stared at each other beneath the bed frame. Layers of silver dust sparkled between us. Shadows hugged his crystal eyes and stained them dark, but a flash of light burst through the iris as we looked at each other.

"Tell me something real, Valen," I said.

The annoyance he sparked inside me melted with his gaze, boiling and simmering into something different, much hotter, much lower.

I swallowed, ignoring the sudden desire his darkened eyes unleashed through me.

"I didn't come here for the Provider." His voice was quiet, slow, leading me to every word. "I came here for —"

A sharp crack exploded through the night. I screamed as shards of sharp crystal rained over me. Several splinters dug into my arms, and part of me realized the glass windowpanes had shattered, but my mind only screamed louder. Panic beat the pain away.

Wood grated against wood. I rolled away from the window, my air too spent to scream again, as a large, dark shape ducked through the opening.

Moonlight framed the figure. Darkness hid all the details of their face. They appeared humanoid, with all the limbs in the right places, but one hand twisted grossly out of shape.

I couldn't see their eyes, but the sudden disturbance in my gut said they looked at me.

"The capital is not welcome here." A deep, male voice said, a hint of gravel in the tones, like its lips didn't quite fit over its teeth.

He stepped closer, that mutilated limb outreached. I scooted backward on my hands and feet. I didn't dare turn away to run. Instincts screamed that putting my back to this intruder would seal my death.

He edged closer, tracking me with eyes like coins the color of night. My back rammed into a solid surface. My pulse increased. I clutched the floor for anything that could help, but the empty hardwood did not yield.

I swallowed thickly. Powerless, that's all I was, again.

The surface against my back moved. I looked up, and up, until the dim moonlight filtering through the window illuminated the blue of his eyes. Valen stood over me, a long silver sword in one hand, staring at the intruder.

"Sorry," Valen said, a hint of humor mixed with that icy anger. "This particularly annoying woman is with me. You're welcome to find another."

The intruder straightened. Valen didn't wait for him to prepare. The mercenary jumped around me, letting me almost fall backward, and arced his sword in a graceful overhead strike.

My jaw dropped. Valen's body moved with an otherworldly fluidity, all power and precision, confidence, and skill. The sword dashed toward the attacker, who skirted back at the last moment. He cried out as the blade bit into his arm, though not the neck strike Valen aimed for. The man stumbled, then rose with the mangled hand lifted. Sharp-tipped claws danced in the pale light.

Valen and the intruder circled each other. Shadows bounced over them, offering glimpses of clarity in the moonlight.

I strained to make out the stranger. He wore dark, flexible clothing, and some kind of cover over the lower part of his face. The visible features were plain, unremarkable.

"Rae!"

Valen and I both swiveled as a familiar voice called my name in the hall. Leof. How did he find me here?

The intruder took advantage of the distraction and launched toward Valen. The mercenary dodged, letting him fall toward the mattress. Wood groaned as the bed frame sagged.

The doorknob jerked roughly, emitting a metallic echo. The wolf's low growl came from the hall, but the deadbolt held. A moment later, the door shook and cried in protest as Leof smacked against it.

The intruder glanced at the door, then at the mercenary slinking closer. Hard resolution filled the few exposed parts of his face.

He looked down at me. "We're not done."

A bang exploded through the room. Splintered wood screamed as remnants of the door tore apart and an angry werewolf snarled from the newly exposed opening. Leof tracked the room. His gaze landed on Valen.

"You!" he roared; his voice mixed with the animal inside him. He leaped across the room, hands twisted into long claws, and slashed at Valen.

"Stop!" I yelled. "Not him, not him!"

Leof paused, Valen's blade caught between twin claws. The intruder ran past the two men and flung himself out the open window.

Everything in the room held still. Leof and Valen remained in frozen combat, before the marshal slowly lowered his claws, and Valen mirrored the action with his sword.

I put my head in my hands and forced a deep breath. "Valen wasn't hurting me. It was the other guy."

"I see that now," Leof said. "But that doesn't explain why you're at the Siren's Sorrow with *him*."

"I'm *investigating*. Why does everyone seem to forget that?"

"But why here?" Leof walked toward me and offered his hand. I took it, ignoring that there had been claws there moments ago. "And why him?" He gestured toward the room.

Which was empty.

"Where . . .?" Leof abandoned me and hurried to the open window. He leaned out, searching the streets.

I didn't bother to look. Valen knew where to find me, and he'd probably show up sooner rather than later.

Leof reached for the sash to close the window.

"Wait!"

He froze, his hand raised. I recovered my bag—somehow stuffed beneath the bed in the commotion—extracted my blade and a second wooden box.

"What?" Leof moved from the window as I took his place. I set the blade against the bone panel I'd placed only hours ago. "Why do you need that?"

"He touched it," I said, as if that explained everything.

"It doesn't have a scent if that's what you're worried about. Must be more wolfsbane."

"That's not what I'm worried about."

Leof nodded. "Of course not. Please, continue to not tell me. I'll just wait outside when you're done."

Chapter 14

Leof and Cherry took me home. Brew would find its own way back.

The horse rocked beneath me. I clutched Leof's thick jacket and rested my cheek against his back. The coldness pressed around us with a bitterness that promised dawn soon. My breath huffed in soft clouds near my lips.

"Tell me, Rae." The first words Leof had spoken since we'd left the Sorrow.

I sighed. The man may still be involved in the murder somehow, but he hadn't attacked us tonight. Besides, it would be more convenient for him to kill me in the depths of the forest, and he didn't seem inclined to do so.

"Is there a reason wolf's prints would be on the planters outside the Siren's Sorrow?" I asked.

"Yeah." Leof's shoulders moved against me. "They're mine."

I raised my head and squinted at the marshal's back. "They're yours?"

"We had a report a couple of weeks ago about some visitors being harassed downtown. The department has rotating shifts to patrol the area every night now. I had duty tonight. That's why I responded so quickly. Why does it matter?"

I leaned back against him. Werewolves ran hot and his warmth bade the chill away. Plus, he felt safe, which seemed rare these days.

"I think whoever threatened the visitors also killed the Provider."

Leof jerked the reins, startling Cherry. He mumbled an apology and patted her neck until she steadied.

"Do you have evidence they're related?"

"Circumstantial. One of the gate guards mentioned a couple were attempting to move from the capital, and the Provider seemed to flee from there as well. I staged a similar story to see if I could persuade the culprit to attack again."

"And that worked so well."

"It worked perfectly. I just didn't think about what to do after the attacker showed up."

"Why would you?" Leof's quiet voice held a hint of humor and frustration. "You didn't tell me about this because you saw the wolf tracks and thought I might be the killer?"

I shrugged. "It was an abundance of caution."

"You don't think I'm the murder anymore?"

"I think you would have killed me by now."

"It's tempting."

We traveled in silence until the oil lanterns dangling from the hooks alongthe streets illuminated the road again. Hints of color lit the sky. Ice crystals danced soft rainbows over the cobblestone streets.

"I brought the glass from the crime scene," Leof said. "I was going to drop it off at your house after my shift."

Despite the exhaustion, a little thrill ran through me. I might have some tangible evidence to lead me to the killer. And once I'd found him, and the Provider left, I could have my life back.

I didn't think about Valen leaving too.

My walkway appeared, branching off the road. Brew perched beside the door, no tracks in the frozen ground, no signs of horses at all.

Leof eyed the wagon. If he had suspicions about its origin, he never asked.

Movement flashed against the lantern light. A short figure moved on my porch and sharpened into Krissa's distinct form. She leaned against the doorjamb with her arms crossed.

"I'd ask to come inside, but I think you have company," Leof said. "And she doesn't look happy."

I sighed. "She's a professor at the college. The rumors about an attack must have made it through town already." Several students likely saw or heard the brawl during whatever unruly nighttime activities young people engaged in.

"Assume everyone knows." Leof slid from the horse, grabbed my satchel from the saddlebag, and pulled out a sealed rectangular box from the adjacent one. "Here's the glass. Let me know what you find."

"If I find anything, you'll be the first person I tell." I glanced at Krissa, waiting for me. "Or maybe the second."

Leof winked, swung onto his horse, and rode into the sunrise.

I pressed my lips together. It turned out friendships were hard. Knowing my actions directly affected someone else gave me an odd itch. I turned toward the house and started forward. Glass jiggled in my bag, but not as much as my heart in my chest.

I reached the porch.

Silence.

"Hi," I whispered.

"You went there without me." Krissa uncrossed, then recrossed her arms. She shifted, her cheeks pink with anger. "You went without me, and I had to hear about it from some drunk college kids! Do you know how embarrassing that was? I kept trying to get answers from them, but they barely remembered how to talk. One of them threw up, and it got on my shoe! My shoe!" She lifted the shoe up. Splashes of questionable liquid shimmered in the light.

"I'm sorry. I made a bad decision."

"And do you know—" She paused. "Wait, what did you say?"

"I said that I'm sorry. I was trying to protect you, and it was stupid. People could have been hurt because I tried to do this alone. I'm not used to working with a partner, but that's not an excuse. I should have told you, and I'm sorry."

Her dark eyes grew wide. The pink color softened, and one side of her lips rose.

"Partner?" she asked.

I raised a brow, hesitant to smile. "If you're willing."

"Oh, hell yes! We're going to solve the crap out of some crimes." She pretended to punch the air. "They'll never see us coming."

Likely because we'd never find them, but I let Krissa celebrate. Her excitement bled into mine.

"I have some evidence to process, if you want to help."

She eyed my bag. "It's in there?"

"Yep."

"What are you waiting for? Let's do this."

I moved past her and opened the door. The wards chimed, settling quickly.

Sure enough, bone fragments littered the living room floor. Bubble half slumped on the couch with his eyes closed, another large piece clutched in his sticky little legs.

"What's this?" Krissa stood next to me.

I didn't have the energy to clean up. I scooted the shards out of the way as I walked to Bubbles and cradled him gently. He didn't move when I took the bone from his foot, or when I carefully placed him on the cushioned bed beside the couch.

"I brought this." Krissa held up a corked bottle of sweet wine.

"Good," I said. "We'll need it."

***

I cleaned off the table, usually reserved for crafting syrups and other ingredients for Brew-Tea-Ful. The three boxes I'd collected through the night replaced the rows of delicate jars and richly colored herbs and tonics.

My kitchen wasn't sentient like Brew, so I hunkered on my hands and knees to search the lowest cupboards. I stacked a couple of votive candles, shallow warming dishes, slim heating stands, and the two largest pots I owned onto the table beside the evidence.

Krissa missed nothing as she watched from the couch beside Bubbles. She sipped her glass of wine, red staining her lips.

"What are you going to do?" she asked.

I placed two stands on the table, with plenty of space between them. One votive candle sat in the center of each stand, and I lit them with my fire striker. The scent of smoke and flame curled around the table.

"If anyone touched these, I'll be able to bring out marks left by their fingers. Everyone has a unique set of marks, called ridges, so if the same person touched these panes or the glass from the crime scene, it'll be enough evidence to connect them to all three events."

"The murder, the threats against the travelers, and the attack on you," Krissa listed. "If you find the killer, can you compare their markings to this evidence, too?"

I smiled. "That's exactly what I can do."

She leaned back again. "Pretty neat."

"Not as neat as math."

She gave a soft laugh.

I dug through my bag from the inn until the jar of white paste appeared. I tilted the jar, letting some of the thick substance ooze into each shallow dish. Once the flow halted, I set the dishes atop the stands. Smoke billowed against the bottom of the dish as the candled warmed the paste. A sharp fish odor followed.

I popped the lid of a container containing yellow-red powder. Scooping some out with a long spoon, I tapped it into a separate dish, then dipped the tips of my fingers into the substance. It clung to my skin, staining them.

"This will let me know which finger markings are my own, so I won't confuse them with any potential suspects."

"That's smart."

I carefully encouraged the original windowpane from its box. Indistinct smudges remained along the top edge, but I couldn't make out any details. I hoped the sticky paste would clarify any remaining details. I leaned the panel against a short wooden block and covered the evidence and the stand with my large pot.

Krissa continued to watch eagerly.

"The candle will heat the adhesive paste I put in the smaller dish. As it warms, the fumes will cover the windowpane. These fumes like to stick to oily substances, and will make them semi-solid, and more easily visible. There's a limited amount of air inside the pot, so hopefully the candle will extinguish before anything becomes too hot."

"Hopefully?" She raised a brow. "Haven't you done this before?"

"Yes, but life happens. It's impossible to control every variable every time. One time I made tea while the paste fumed. I ended up spilling my kettle and water soaked the bottom of the evidence. Needless to say, the process wasn't as successful that time."

"How long does it take?"

I shrugged. "I'll check it in a half hour or so."

"Plenty of time for you to tell me everything. I'm assuming you warded the house against unwanted listeners?"

I wrung my fingers. I wished there was something else for me to do, but I only had two stands and we both already had drinks.

The warm stone of the hearth soaked into my legs as I sat across from Krissa. I'd called her a friend more than once these past few days. One of the few things I knew of friendship was that it required honesty.

"Ask me anything."

"You're actually from the capital, not just near it."

I nodded. "I lived there since my first memories."

"What did you do there?" She phrased it as a question, but those dark eyes admitted she already knew.

I waved my hand over the tattoo on my wrist. The masking spell wore away, revealing the sharp lines of the Provider's dagger.

Krissa sipped her wine. I lifted mine to my lips as well, letting the sweet, fruity drink warm my gut.

"How long?"

"I left five years ago. I served the king for over twenty years."

"Your parents?"

I shook my head. "I don't remember them. For a while, I lived in the castle's nursery, cared for by the nurses of the royal family. Once my magic started manifesting, I lived and trained with the Providers."

"You're a necromancer."

The words cut sharper than I expected. My heart fluttered in my chest. That's what they had called me for years. Not my given name, nor my chosen one, but the King's Necromancer. Memories tried to rise, but I forced them down.

"Yes."

"They trained you?"

"Yes, and no. They trained me to do one particular task, under extreme supervision, and forbade me to learn any more of my abilities. The king feared what I may do if I learned them."

Krissa lowered her voice to a whisper. "What was it? What did you do for him?"

I bit my lip. Our fragile friendship may dissolve from the truth, at the depths of the horrible things I'd done. She'd have enough information to turn me into the king and the Providers would drag me back.

But . . . I'd been alone for so long. I needed to tell someone the truth, craved to have this secret finally revealed.

"Necromancers were hunted to almost extinction long ago for the threat they posed against the capital. But then, the king discovered he was sick, slowly dying. Suddenly, the one magic he'd almost eliminated became what he needed to survive. But eventually he found me."

I didn't remember my parents. Maybe he'd had a mage hide the memories, or my mind shielded me from the ones too painful to remember. But I liked to think they fought for me when the king's men arrived. That they'd loved me enough to die for me.

My throat clenched. I swallowed. The truth was thicker than I'd expected.

"They taught me to manipulate life forces. I could take the life from a young, healthy subject and give it to something sick or aging. The forces were never equal. A transfer added a handful of years to the other's life, but not enough for a whole lifespan. At first, they brought me animals, healthy and sick. Once I'd mastered the skill, it became people."

Krissa kept her face flat. "You gave the king longer to live, by taking life from others."

"Yes. They claimed the subjects were criminals from the dungeons, and I was too ingrained to ask many questions at that point. Lack of performance or any perceived insubordination resulted in painful beatings. I learned to be quiet."

"How did you escape?"

I felt the dark smile on my lips. "At one training lesson, they brought in a man bound in chains and another that was basically a breathing shell. I was still recovering from a previous punishment. My magic was hungry for revenge, but all I had was obedience. And then I realized I had more."

I closed my eyes, and the memories I'd tried to repress flooded back.

The room in the tower of the castle, only below where the archers perched and secured the wall's defenses. Hard stone beneath my feet. The conflicting rise and fall of my thoughts as I considered my mission, my purpose in life. As I realized death always found me.

Chains rattled as the guards dragged the man in. Another followed, carried by four more guards, and placed on his back in the center of the room.

"Begin," the Provider behind me said. He wore his hood up to shadow his face, the same way I wore mine.

Bruises covered my hands as I raised them, despite the protest of sore muscles. Visibility diminished in my left eye as the swelling forced the lid mostly closed.

My magic rose, hot and angry, happy for an outlet. It circled around the bound man, eagerly feeling his youth, his life, and craving to take it as my own.

He met my gaze. A fire burned in his eyes.

I froze. They never looked at me. Begged, pleaded, bargained, but never stared quietly, a sharp defiance so visible.

He didn't look like a prisoner. Healthy muscles circled his arms and legs. His face was full, a rich color to his cheeks. I'd seen others half wasted away, a sort of madness in their expressions. Healthy, yes, young, yes, but not like this man.

It didn't surprise me that the Providers had lied. It surprised me that I'd so easily believed them.

All that hot anger seeped into my power. I let it flood the room, let the Provider feel I obeyed. The guards shifted, uncomfortable with the heat or their role, I never knew.

I pulled. All that power, that glorious knowledge they'd given me, fed happily on the life in the room.

Except I didn't take from the man watching me so calmly. No, I trapped the Provider, all the guards, even the weak patient, unable to move or speak, in the thick net of my power. I pulled again, drowning their voices first, and again, taking their breath, their heartbeats, the heat from their bodies.

Their mouths opened in silent screams. My laughter became the only sound in the room.

When they finally collapsed to the ground, I held the power of seven lives in my hands. The desire for more overwhelmed me. I could take their lives. Could level the castle with it. I could kill and kill and kill.

Or . . . I could leave. This power didn't feel good. It felt molten and dangerous, poison disguised with sugar. I was so tired of death.

The man stood. His shackles jingled.

"I can help," he whispered.

I caught his gaze again.

"And you will." My words were not a request. They demanded everything from him. I gathered all that power and pushed it into

him. His face twisted. The spark in his eyes faded, replaced with something else.

My will.

He rose. The chains shattered from his wrists. The strength of seven lives inside him at once would be too much for his body to sustain for long.

But I didn't need him for long. I only needed him to get me out of this castle, out of this city.

He wouldn't survive. But I would.

I opened my eyes again.

"I did terrible things while I was there, and terrible things to escape. Helping Leof, learning everything I can about my specific knowledge can benefit us, can benefit society. It felt like I could redeem myself somehow. But lately, I realized I needed out completely. I need to focus on life instead."

Krissa pursed her lips. "Rae, you could kill the king. You could train your magic, raise an army of supporters, march on the capital and kill the man responsible for so much pain."

"You don't understand." I raised my tattoo. "This mark is a direct connection to the king. Any time I use my necromancy powers, he'd feel it immediately. If I tried to practice, he'd be here in a heartbeat, and would erase any sign I'd ever been here. That's why I have to use potions and common magic—to avoid being found. It's better for me, for Hollow's Promise, if I keep hiding."

She let the silence settle for a moment.

"You can't hide forever," she said, softly.

"I can try."

She chuckled, but not with a hint of pleasure. "It sounds like you're really screwed, Rae."

Maybe it was the wine, or the company, but I laughed. Krissa raised her brows, took another sip of her drink, and joined in.

She was right, though. I was screwed.

Chapter 15

The southern portion of Hallow's Promise was officially called Glory Gardens but had long ago received the nickname the Chopines. Chopines were a high shoe, designed to keep mud off the feet of high-status women, and almost everyone that lived in Glory Gardens assumed we were the mud to be stepped on. Continuing north from the Chopines, each neighborhood fell a little in wealth and prestige, until the north side of the town which contained smaller clusters of simple homes where multiple generations shared one or two roomed cottages. And a few areas of slums lined the northern wall.

Main Street cut across the center of Hallow's Promise, and the Sherriff's Station sat at the intersection of Main and Swear. Close enough to the downtown affairs, but far enough that the lack of upkeep didn't affect the appeal of Main Street. The Station boasted a whitewashed stone exterior, and an even more boring bleached interior. The holding cells sat beneath the ground floor, so the unruly remained hidden from visitors. A little desk perched at the entryway. I'd never seen anyone sit at it.

After the glue finished fuming, I'd carefully sketched each print I'd discovered on the evidence items. At the areas with similar markings, I'd painted colored dots to visualize the matching locations. The actual items remained at home. Brew and Bubbles waited nearby, along the closest ley line.

I turned a corner and ran into something hard and too warm to be a wall. A squeal escaped my throat as I tumbled forward, right over another person heading face-first into the ground as well.

Castor landed more gracefully than I did, which made my jaw clench. My arms and legs tangled with the slow cascade of paperwork while the constable caught himself with his hands and the balls of his feet.

My head hit the ground. Ouch.

Castor paused for a moment. His icy eyes surveyed the layer of parchment scattered on the hall floor. His hands balled into fists as he turned to me.

I swallowed. "Hi."

"You are the only one that could have made this day worse."

Gee, thanks. I rolled onto my knees and stood up. Nothing seemed too injured, except a minor ache at the back of my head. I pressed my fingers into my hair and drew them back. No blood, good.

"I didn't really want to see you either." I flinched at how weak the words sounded.

Castor smirked. "I see the werewolf has lost his pet witch. Are you bringing him a tonic for a tummy ache?"

I smiled, a little too sweetly. "Actually, I came to offer you a growth potion. With such an inflated ego, I imagine you're compensating for something much smaller."

His brow creased a moment before his face turned red.

"I do not need—"

"Castor!" Leof's voice boomed down the hall. He circled one of the arched doorways and paused when he saw us. The marshal recovered quickly—two adults sprawled in a pile of parchment not even worth commenting on. "You should be at the Shrine District by now. I gave your assignment hours ago."

Castor gave his superior a sharp nod, even as his expression tried to shoot daggers at the larger man. "I had to gather some information first."

"You have one minute to get out of this station." He turned to me, that ferocity still trapped in his gaze. "And you, come into my office."

He turned and disappeared.

Castor mumbled under his breath as he scooped the papers into a pile. I mimicked him, scanning the mess for my pages and shuffling them into a haphazard stack. All three fingerprint sketches, plus the extras I'd made for Leof, accounted for.

In fact, an extra page peeked from my pile. I urged the parchment out, tipping it toward the lantern light.

Erline Case # 22 Suicide–Closed sprawled in thick penmanship across the top.

Suicide? At the capital? If the case was closed, why did Castor have stacks of information about it?

A shadow covered the page.

"That's mine." Castor's voice lowered, a hint of an echo beneath it.

I tried to hide my shaking fingers as I persuaded the page from the others. I plastered on a thick smile, attempting to keep my face flat and innocent, and handed the page back.

"Sorry about that," I heard myself say, as my mind tried to fit round puzzle pieces into square holes. "It got mixed in my things."

Castor snatched the page and remained silent as he stalked down the hall. I waited for his footsteps to fade before standing, feeling even more confused.

Leof's office wasn't large, but a tall window invited natural light and made the space feel bigger. A long desk sat against one wall, with a stout wooden chair pushed against it. Parchments, wax melts, and an assortment of other stationery scattered over the surface.

Two leather chairs and a low table filled most of the center of the room. If Leof had been a potion master, this room would be his cauldron. He thought best in here, brought in criminals, sat them down in the plush leather chairs, gave them a sympathetic ear, and they spilled their guts. He'd solved murders, kidnappings, and countless other crimes from the comfort of these twin chairs.

A trio of candles clustered at the center of the table. Last time I visited, they had been light and fresh scents, but today they smelled like pumpkin and the first winter's snow.

The Leof perched in his favorite chair—the one nearest the window—looking completely different from the angry marshal moments before. He'd undone the top button of his tunic, removed his simple leather shoes, and bit into a wedge of cheese—no crackers in sight.

He held the chewed wedge out. "Want some?"

"Maybe next time." I slid into the open chair. The delicate, earthy, old leather greeted me with a snug embrace. I turned sideways to see the werewolf better and drew my feet over the arm of the chair. With the sunlight streaming on my face, a nap sounded awfully tempting.

"What did you find?" Leof asked.

I flicked through the pages and handed him the detailed sketches. His dark eyes traveled over the pages without a suggestion of emotion.

He looked at me. "This is from—"

"Yes."

"All of them."

"The same person."

He flicked the pages onto the table, managing to perfectly avoid the candles. He snapped up and paced toward a tower bookshelf across the room.

"Damn, yes, Rae! Yes! This is a major development. This could solve our case!"

I smiled. "If we find a suspect with the same prints, it will solve our case."

Leof stopped pacing. He put his head in his hands. "I sent Suzie to her mother's house."

I flinched. I knew how much they loathed each other. Leof fought hard for Suzie to stay with him when she was a child, but Ellen won every time. When Suzie moved to Hallow's Promise for college, Leof was overjoyed. Sending her away, even temporarily, must hurt—but it kept her safe.

"We'll find them, Leof. We can find them before the deadline, and we can put this behind us."

"I think you might be right," he said.

I let the moment of relief settle around us, then broke it.

"Hey, is there a reason Castor would have information about a suicide case from the capital?"

Leof's brow pinched. "He requested some paperwork about Gerrin's brother, but there wasn't a case. It was a cut and clear suicide. He had a history of illness, previous attempts, and he wrote a note found in his residence. There wasn't an investigation."

"Castor had a lot of parchments that appeared otherwise."

Leof shrugged. "I let my marshals assist other towns if there's a request. Maybe someone asked him for help."

"Hm." I let the thought fumble in my mind. It didn't fit quite right. And the Provider's death being a staged suicide, while Gerrin's brother apparently died the same way, seemed too convenient.

A dark feeling twisted in my gut. Too many coincidences, too many explanations.

"There's seven days left. What's your plan?" Leof interrupted my thoughts.

"*My* plan?" I raised my brows. "You're the trained professional."

Leof waved the words away. "Do you know why I brought you onto that first case when you'd barely arrived at Hallow's Promise?"

"I assumed you could sense my magic, since I wasn't as good at shielding it."

The wolf shook his head. "No, it wasn't because of your magic. It only took a few minutes of talking to you to know you see the world differently. There isn't black and white. There's every shade in-between."

A deep discomfort settled in my gut, and I resisted twisting in my seat. "You don't know what I think, Leof."

"I know it's good, Rae—that you're good."

I stood up. My papers fluttered to the ground for the second time today. I snatched them up and handed Leof his simpler sketches.

"These are yours," I said. "I'm leaving."

"Where are you going?"

I didn't pause as I exited his office. "Apparently it doesn't matter how you see the world; you still have to make money to survive."

The door snapped shut.

***

Brew's floorboards crunched and popped with every step I took. My jaw ached from the tight clench I'd maintained most of the afternoon. Even Bubbles couldn't sleep with the constant noises—which meant it was really loud. He stared up at me, a bit exasperated, and thumped his back feet in a snappy rhythm.

"You can keep the change," the mage student said as I exchanged the enchanted tonic for their coins. Another customer replaced them immediately.

"The Sustainabili-TEA please," she ordered. The same drink, probably the tenth time in a row. I'd forgotten about exam schedules. If I'd been here all week, I wouldn't have to worry about money.

I smiled. "It'll be a moment."

The water heated over the oven, and I reached for the dried herb drawer. Brew snapped it shut, and I barely avoided having my fingers smashed.

I bent down and opened a lower cupboard, pretending to search inside, and dropped my voice.

"Listen," I poked my finger into the wagon's frame and the floor creaked menacingly. "I know we don't have much time to figure out this case, but I don't have anywhere to look next. And if we don't make some money, I won't be able to afford to feed Bubbles. Is that what you want?" I gestured to the warplog. "Do you want him to starve?"

The wagon's resignation turned the air heavy. I patted the cupboard door. "Me too, Brew. Me too."

When I stood up, the herb drawer remained open.

I plucked a healthy spring of dried rosemary and set it on a granite slab beside the basin. A swift flick of a match and the rosemary caught a healthy, golden flame. Before too much smoke saturated the wagon, I flipped a glass over the top and let the rich smoke dwell inside. The smokey texture demanded a strong companion flavor, which paired well with the fruity strength of cranberry tea.

I grabbed a teapot and measured a few spoonfuls of my favorite cranberry citrus mixture into the depths.

Castor offering to help anyone except himself seemed laughable. There wasn't a reason he'd take on another department's case, especially one already closed. It stunk of an ulterior motive.

The kettle perked atop the flames, and I drew it off. Steam billowed into the kettle as the citrus fruit flavors combined. Partnered with the lingering rosemary smoke, the flavors in the air tasted almost as good as the tea. I added a healthy amount of simple syrup and capped the top while it seeped.

The initials pressed into the body were strange as well. They were small, with a deeper circle impressed around them, like a stamp of some sort.

I flipped the smoke cup right-side up and pressed a thin cloth filter into its rim. I poured the tea slowly, catching the spent leaves and letting the smoke remnants settle into the liquid. Once it all poured, I squeezed an orange wedge over the top.

What required an initialed stamp . . .

I cradled the drink in both hands and let the warmth flow through me. My magic uncurled slightly, enough to press a light energy spell into the drink, then it relaxed again. The king couldn't detect casual magic usage.

"Here you are." I passed the drink through the sash. The woman reached for it, a flash of midday sun highlighting a silver ring on her hand.

I paused.

The king had a ring very similar. How many times had I seen a silver flash like that in the echoes of torchlight while I passed the life of one into another?

His had borne the royal crest, but also his personal three letters in the center.

CRG. It was a seal.

"Um, can I have my drink, please?"

I jumped. "Oh, I'm so sorry. Yes, here, please enjoy." The woman handed me her coins and disappeared deeper into the campus.

"Sorry!" I yelled, not bothering to look at the next customers. "I have to close early!"

A chorus of complaints came from outside, but Brew snapped the sash shut. The faint sound of the sash locking told me Brew knew I'd had a revelation.

I packed up my supplies. Drawers and cupboards opened before I reached for them. "It's an insignia ring. Those letters are initials, possibly the killer's! We have to go tell Leof." Who'd probably already realized the origin of the impression.

I slowed my packing. There was one person too interested in the case, and very committed to attempting to ward me away. And at least one of his initials matched.

Castor.

Maybe I couldn't tell Leof yet. Even if he disliked the man, Leof trusted his people explicitly. I needed more than one random letter and a hunch. I needed—

My wards screamed inside my head, clanging bells attempting to rip my skull apart. I grabbed my forehead and kneeled, gasping for air.

Something had broken into my house.

Something terrible.

Chapter 16

Brew took us home as fast as possible. A headache pounded low in my skull. The wards weren't just broken—someone obliterated them. A faint echo where they used to be pulsed hollowly in my brain.

The wagon stopped its subtle motion of ley line travel, and I hurried to the rear door. I fumbled with the latch, my hands heavy and slow. Brew popped it for me.

Daylight streamed into the wagon. I blinked, and a shadow crowded the opening. Leof held one end of the door, stopping it from opening all the way.

"How bad?" I asked.

His tight expression told me everything. A heaviness hung low in my heart. I tried to push the door open, but he held it tight.

"I need to see," I said.

"Let me and my guys clean it up some. You don't need to see your home like this."

The thumping in my head grew stronger. "Let me out."

"Rae—"

Another figure appeared, wider and taller than the werewolf.

"She said move." Valen's voice sounded low, a sharp edge slithering under the words. That cool rage billowed beneath the surface.

Leof tensed. "I told you to leave. You don't belong here."

Violence ran between the men, as fragile as a glass cane, waiting for the strike that would shatter them both.

Valen stepped closer. He spoke to the wolf, but he looked at me. Shadows gathered in his gaze, an intensity that awoke instincts deep in my gut that a predator stalked me and morning may not arrive soon enough.

"It's her home. If she wants to see it, she sees it."

Leof turned toward the man. Brew snapped the door open, and I slipped out behind the wolf's back. He seemed too distracted to notice, but Valen watched my every move over the marshal's shoulder.

The two could fight if they wanted. My world narrowed into the maw of my broken front door.

The wood panel hung on the lower hinge; the top corner propped against a windowpane cradling remnants of shattered glass. Shards crunched beneath my feet as I stepped through the entry. Inside, two constables stilled as I entered, but I barely saw them.

I froze.

My eyes took in the damage, the ruins, but my mind refused to understand the image. I tried to reconcile how the space looked this morning compared to the mess it resembled now.

The couch where Krissa and I shared wine and dismantled secrets. Cushions torn from the structure and sliced into pieces. The wooden frame splintered down the center and rested on its back, the empty bench staring at the ceiling.

Every cupboard and drawer gaped open, some of the doors ripped from their hinges. My stock potions, syrups, herbs, and glasses shattered into a pile in the center. A disgusting yellow liquid cascaded from the pile. Years of work trashed and pissed on. The kitchen table bore long gashes, the sharp edge of some kind of axe or hatchet clear in the grooves.

Two scents mixed, a sort of terrible cocktail of sharp urine and bitter smoke.

Someone stepped beside me. Valen, a silent shadow.

I walked to the stairs. I thought the mercenary would attempt to stop me, but he only followed.

My clothes layered the loft in a shredded mess. They'd tried to light the bed on fire, but the flames had either been contained, or the material proved inflammable. A blessing, perhaps, that my entire home hadn't burned to the ground, but one I felt too numb to appreciate.

My knees shook as the shock slowly wore into grief. Leaving the capital was supposed to offer me a new chance, a life safe from threats and danger. Working with Leof had never put me at risk before—most criminals didn't look at the world beyond themselves. Whoever did this harbored a deep, evil, intelligence and motivation.

I sank to the ground. My clothes—all chopped or shredded—cushioned me while I leaned against the loft banister.

Valen sat beside me. The coolness still settled in his face, but he felt warm against my side.

"This is my home," I whispered.

He watched me, waiting.

"I put everything into this. I made it something my past could never touch." The words would be meaningless to the mercenary, but I didn't care. "I earned this myself. And someone came in here and tried to take it all away."

The shock, the sadness sank below the surface. It didn't fade, didn't leave, but a different emotion overwhelmed them both—a stronger one.

The fire inside me raged hotter than I'd ever felt. My magic responded, all life and death, and the temptation to use it burned.

"What do you want to do?" Valen asked.

I raised my chin. "I want to find who did this."

"And?"

Valen was an unknown. He worked for the Provider ordering me to deliver the murderer to the capital. The culprit would surely meet a terrible fate if I complied, but it lacked the personal punishment I craved. The man had attacked me at the Siren's Sorrow, figured out where I lived, shattered my life's work, and literally pissed all over it.

My hands clenched into fists. If me, Bubbles, or Brew had been here, we wouldn't have survived. We'd be the next case on Leof's desk.

"I'll make sure they can never hurt anyone again." It was my voice, but someone else spoke the words, someone deep inside my magic, where death and life only meant power I could control.

Valen smiled. The darkness leached from that expression, a hunger my magic recognized, but didn't know.

"I'll help," he said.

***

Gerrin and a constable I didn't recognize lingered in the living area. They looked at me, then glanced away uncomfortably.

Valen didn't leave my side as we walked through the house. I kept my stare forward, avoiding the remains of my belongings in the room.

Gerrin touched my arm as I passed.

"I'm so sorry. I hope they didn't take anything valuable."

I hesitated. I'd been so shocked by the state of the house, I hadn't thought to see if anything was missing.

And of course it was. Where the sharp lines on the kitchen table resided now, had been the tiles of evidence I'd collected from the Siren's Sorrow. My detailed sketch documents were also missing. All I had left from days of investigating this case were the simple fingerprint outlines I'd given Leof.

The loss didn't ripple my emotions. The numbness soaked too deep.

"Do you need any help?" The constable still talked to me.

"No, thank you." I looked around the room, where all three constables watched me as carefully as a case of fire-pox. "You can all go."

The two constables shuffled out, but Leof lingered. "I'll finish the investigation before the Provider returns. You don't have to worry about it anymore."

I put my hand on my friend's arm. He meant well, and Leof would do almost anything for me, but he kept his mind on the law. And I didn't want to.

"She said you can go," Valen repeated, low and harsh beside me.

Leof raised a brow, but when I remained quiet, the wolf turned and left.

I gave them a few moments and went to the doorway. The three spoke quietly at the edge of the drive. Then they mounted their horses and rode away.

The quiet felt good. It fed my rage.

"We need to make a plan," I said. "But first, we need to pick someone up."

Chapter 17

Most of the forest accepted its conversion into urban development at the formation of Hallow's Promise. A few chunks remained, strategically placed around the city to offset clusters of houses. Spirit's Peak, the mountain that juts through the west side of the wall, harboring thick groves that shed brown pine needles across half of the town.

The Void was a dense cluster of tress near the North gate that did not accept civilization. Settled opposite the poorest strip of the city, The Void grew thicker and darker than a regular forest. It ate up any structures too close to the perimeter, including the road, which had to be replaced once or twice a year. Where a regular forest may house rodents or stags, The Void's creatures had a lot more teeth.

I'd set Brew just inside the borders of The Void. Multiple candles lit the interior of the wagon, but the darkness still pressed against us. A witch, a mercenary, and a magic wagon should have a chance against the creatures sulking in the shadows. Krissa could probably tell us our odds of survival.

But more than the foreboding sense of danger, nobody would look for us in The Void. It offered the perfect place for illicit planning.

Krissa and Valen sat in the back of my wagon, side-by-side, their backs pressed against the latched door. The sight would have been comical any other time. Valen seemed just as secure brooding in the wagon as he did threatening people outside. Krissa wrapped her skirts around her legs, the rainbow colors in sheer contrast to Valen's all black ensemble. She wore those twin braids again, with ribbons hanging longer than her locks.

They both watched me. Krissa appeared concerned, her brows a bit creased, her lips pressed together. Valen looked too happy.

The lit oven made sweat bead on my face, and I let it run down my nose. A concoction of apples and cinnamon boiled over the flames, filling the wagon with the scent of a lingering fall. I pressed the juicer shut on a fat orange and squeezed, satisfaction escaping with every drop the fruit released.

"They took the evidence?" Krissa asked. She'd tried to initiate the conversation multiple times, but I hadn't been ready yet.

I was ready now.

"And they destroyed my house."

She nodded. "And they destroyed your house."

"We're going to find them and make sure they understand exactly what a poor decision that was," Valen chimed in.

Krissa waved at him. "Yes, yes, a broody and melancholy thirst for violence over here, I get it. But putting that aside, *how* are we going to find him? We don't have any evidence. The only lead is three letters found in a mark on the body that may or may not be related, and the murderer is using wolfsbane to hide his scent."

I set a large bowl in the basin and placed a colander on top. My arms shook as I heaved the apple cider into the strainer. Chunks of fruit caught inside, the precious juice collecting in the bowl.

I set the apples on the countertop to cool and scooped most of the juice into three hearty mugs.

"I have an idea about who might be involved," I said.

Both of them straightened.

"Are you going to share?" Krissa crossed her arms.

Brew popped open an upper cupboard. If the wagon gathered dust, this cupboard would bear a hefty layer. I stood on my tiptoes and pulled out a bottle of distilled alcohol, purchased long ago from a foreign market for a steep price. A tiny etching of juniper berries dug into the glass bottle. The delicate flavor paired perfectly with the cider, creating a delicious drink that hopefully stoked the dedication inside me.

I didn't measure the booze as I poured.

"Here." I passed out the mugs. Neither of them questioned me as they pressed the drink to their lips. "Whoever killed the Provider knew enough to make it look like a suicide. Only Leof's instincts made him investigate further."

"They're either familiar with the tactics or did some careful research," Krissa said.

I nodded. "And they covered their tracks with wolfsbane, which isn't easy to get."

"They might have ties to the underground markets." Valen's gaze darkened.

"That's something to consider, but there are other ways to get a hold of it."

"Only healers and sheriff's stations have access to wolfsbane because of its poisonous nature," Krissa said. "They use it for tonics or subduing violent criminals." Her eyes widened. "Are you saying—"

"Yes. I think the murderer got the wolfsbane legally." I drew a deep breath. "I think it's Leof's corporal—Castor."

"Castor?" Krissa crinkled her nose. "He's the one that you said was mean to you."

"He seemed to hate me right away, and I thought it was because Leof brought an outsider into another one of his cases. But maybe he saw me as a threat to his plans. The initials left in an imprint on the body are CRG. Castor's name fits."

"It fits one letter," Valen said. "What are his other names?"

"I don't know, but I'm going to find evidence to prove he did it."

"How?"

"By breaking into his house and finding something with his fingerprints. Then I can compare them to the sketches I gave to Leof."

Valen crossed his arms. "Do you know where he lives?"

I pointed a thumb over my shoulder toward the steaming liquid trapped in the bowl at the bottom of the basin.

"That's what the cider is for."

***

I spread a map of Hallow's Promise over the only countertop wide enough to hold it. The pages stared up in a familiar pattern. The four main roads curved around the edges of the city and met in careful points at each corner.

I ran my finger along the tiny western road that ventured toward my house. I'd walked the path so many times, I could navigate it with my eyes closed.

Home.

Wrecked.

My fingers curled into an unwilling fist. Magic and anger never mixed well. It often produced unintended consequences, something darker and more twisted than desired. But occasionally, anger fueled the magic and turned it more powerful. We'd find out which happened tonight.

Krissa looked over my shoulder. "Is this part of the spell?"

"No, sorry, I got distracted."

"Oh." She leaned back.

Valen spoke from the rear corner, where he held up the wagon with one shoulder. "You can't use a location spell to track a person. They only find objects you've marked."

"Or touched," I smiled.

His brow creased. "It's much more difficult."

"You have no idea how difficult I can be."

"I think I do."

The response didn't merit a reply. Instead, I gathered the glass bowl from the basin. The warmth from the mixture sank into my palms. My hands didn't shake, which I took as a good sign since I hadn't performed this spell in quite a while.

"I thought you couldn't use magic . . ." Krissa trailed off with a subtle glance toward Valen.

I dropped my voice, but it didn't particularly matter. If Brew didn't want Valen to hear, he wouldn't. "I can't use specific parts of my magic, or anything with a lot of power. But a simple locating spell like this will be fine. The potion will do most of the heavy lifting, anyway."

The bowl swirled at my light touch. Specks of deep cinnamon blended into the rich amber fluid. I let my magic gather inside me.

"Where did you learn all this, if your upbringing was so . . . specific?"

"When I left, I realized how little I knew about the world. I decided never to be in that place again. I started visiting every library I passed, reading as many books as I could." And sleeping in the hallways or outside the doors, though I refused to reveal that. "Books gave me a different power: research and science."

Valen jutted into the conversation. "So, you started studying death?"

I shrugged. "I found out a lot of my skills helped people. Turns out, most of those people are already dead." I theorized that my magic called to death, and a natural affinity sharpened otherwise innate skills. But it was only a theory.

"I'll need it to be silent."

Brew tuned in with my power. A soft wind blew through the wagon, extinguishing several of the candles until a gentle golden glow illuminated the space. The map remained bright enough to see.

I closed my eyes. The cider was both delicious—and magic. I'd spent years tracking down the right trees, generations separated from the apple of Eden itself. The priestess of Goliath—a primordial water god—had blessed the water. Even the cinnamon contained special qualities, as it had been harbored inside Brew's spice cupboard, exposed to the wagon's unique magic.

Together, they formed the foundation of a powerful searching spell.

I let a wisp of my power sink into the liquid as I swirled it in my palms. Only a little slipped into the liquid, enough to expose the magical properties within the brew. Krissa gasped. I didn't look, but I knew the concoction had burst into a silver light.

Valen had been right. A regular locating spell required a special mark on the item it tracked. But this potion enhanced the magic enough to search and find my touch on an object. And when I'd helped Castor clean up his papers outside Leof's office, I'd touch a lot of them.

With a final soft push of power, I spilled the entire bowl over the map. I paused at the end, giving every drop an opportunity to escape from the glass. When the press and pull of my magic slowed, then stopped, I opened my eyes.

Liquid pooled on the parchment. Ink bled where thicker areas of cider gathered. Cinnamon speckled the paper and turned it a smokey orange color. Cider soaked the map.

Except one circular spot.

Valen abandoned his post. The three of us leaned over the map, peering at the last remaining dry section of Hallow's Promise.

The edge of East Brim, across the street from the Sherriff's Station.

"Good job, Sunshine," Valen said, and I didn't correct him.

Chapter 18

Krissa fared better after her second experience traveling with Brew. She only swayed for a couple minutes, and her face barely turned green. Valen strode from the door without a second thought, like he traveled the ley lines all the time.

I shut the door and waited for the latch to snap on the lock. Bubbles and Brew would be safe. I could only hope for the rest of us.

The wagon vibrated. I rested my forehead on its doorway.

"I'll be okay," I whispered. Brew shuttered, concerned or comforting, maybe both.

Breaking into a potential killer's house—who was also a trailed city constable—was a bad idea on a good day. I certainly wasn't having a good day.

For the past five years, I'd avoided taking unnecessary risks. I kept my head down, sold my potions, and set my wards every day. Now, a Provider hovered over me with the ghosts of my past, a dangerous mercenary called me Sunshine, and I had people I cared about losing. A fist clenched in my chest, each finger a reminder of what we risked.

Krissa put her hand on my shoulder. "Are you okay?"

Her touch comforted me. I didn't want to go back to my old life. I probably couldn't sleep without Bubble's soft snores now. I enjoyed making Krissa tea whenever she showed up. Leof trusted me, more than I'd ever realized. Even Valen had become tolerable.

I lifted my head from the wagon and smiled. "I'm fine. Let's do this."

Valen led the way into the shadows. Most of Hallow's Promise had accepted the late hour. Darkness shone through windows, an occasional flash of warming fires. He guided us gently right, around the edge of the college, away from the Sherriff's Station.

The houses thinned as we entered the East Brim. Properties grew wider, areas of farmland consuming large swaths. The quietness of the city faded, replaced by chirping frogs, groaning cattle, and an occasional mysterious sound I didn't want to identify.

A short house appeared from the depths. Whitewashed stonework built into a single-floor home with a sharp, thatched roof. Bone-lined windows offered little visibility into the residence, except for an occasional sharp flicker of a candle dancing between the panes.

Valen held his hand up before we reached the property line.

"Someone's inside," he said.

"Maybe Castor is awake?" I offered.

Valen shook his head, an almost unperceivable gesture. "You don't sulk by candlelight through your own house."

I studied the motions of the light. It moved slowly, precisely, occasionally dimming as something obscured it. The pattern did appear odd. Almost like the holder lacked confidence in their motions. Not a comfortable pace for a resident.

"Let's get a little closer." The mercenary waved us forward.

Every crunch of grass against our feet made my heart beat faster. Maybe I had been wrong the whole time. Maybe Castor had become the killer's next victim.

The house loomed as we approached. The soft scent of lavender from a nearby garden drifted on a cold breeze. It reminded me of lavender syrup, the kind I used frequently in potions, the kind I'd have to remake from scratch because the killer had ruined all my supplies.

I needed to know if it was Castor. I didn't have any other options.

Valen pointed toward a flat area of ground between two windows. We half slouched, half crawled toward it, until the cool stones of the house pressed into my back. I felt my heart in the bottom of my throat. Sweat coated my palms.

Valen pointed up, and I followed the gesture. The slight illumination from inside the house revealed shattered bone panels hanging in the frame. I glanced at the ground beneath the sill, squinting in the faint moonlight. The ground remained clear. Whoever broke the shards had picked them up to hide the evidence.

Sharp blue eyes caught my gaze. Valen studied my face for a moment. His lips parted, then he winked at me and dove through the shattered window.

I froze. Krissa gasped beside me. My mind tried to comprehend that the man leapt through the window toward an unknown, potentially dangerous, individual.

"Do we . . . follow?" Krissa whispered.

I did a hard blink and shrugged.

Crashes exploded from the inside. Distinct male grunts echoed, followed by several more concerning crunching noises. I popped to my feet, heading toward the window to see if Valen wanted me to enter.

"You guys can come in now," the mercenary called.

I peeked my head through the hole. Valen had another man in a chokehold. The dark-shrouded stranger gasped in thick breaths around the grip.

"I unlocked the door," Valen said.

Krissa and I edged our way around the building to the front door. It opened with a slight twist, spilling us into a wide living area. A fire had long gone cold, and an almost icy chill hugged the entire house. It didn't feel creepy—it felt lonely.

We met Valen at the rear of the house, which contained a standard kitchen and eating area. A squat table near the back wall lay flipped over, and one of the two chairs missed a leg.

"Any idea who this is?" Valen swung the culprit around, putting his face into the light of the single candle.

"Gerrin!" I yelled, "Valen, let him go!"

His grip loosened only slightly. "Why? He broke into someone's house."

"Well, so did we," I stammered. "He's one of Leof's constables. The marshal will be livid if you hurt him."

Valen dropped his arms and Gerrin fell to the floor, one hand clutching his throat, the other pressed against a bloody nose.

He looked up at me. "Rae?" He coughed. "What are you doing here?"

"What are *you* doing here?" Krissa asked, her arms crossed.

Gerrin got to his knees but paused there with a side glance at the mercenary.

"I . . . had a really dumb thought, and I decided to check it out." He scratched the back of his neck with one hand, studying the floor with a harsh gaze.

I kneeled beside him. "Did you think Castor might be the killer?"

Gerrin looked at me, his eyes wide. "How did you know?"

"Why do you think we're here?"

"You have suspicions, too? I thought my imagination was getting the best of me."

Valen pulled out the unbroken chair. "Why don't you tell us what you think?"

Gerrin's knees wobbled a bit, but he sat down. The mercenary hovered over him.

"It really starts with my brother's death. The capital determined that he . . . killed himself, but I couldn't understand how he could do that. I tried to accept it, even talked myself into it for a while. But then, this Provider looked like he'd killed himself and it ended up being a murder. I wondered if that could have happened to him, too."

Gerrin's face gained some more color while he spoke.

"I requested the case notes from the capital archives, but I never received them. When I checked with the messengers weeks later, they said someone already collected the records. I asked who picked up the files, but they refused to tell me. I might have spiraled a little bit and ended up in Leof's office for a reprimand. As I left, I saw Castor next door—and the papers in his hand said my brother's name."

"That means he murdered him?"

Gerrin shrugged. "I didn't know what it meant, but it made me suspicious. I wanted to search here while Castor was on a night shift. I figured he'd either have proof of the murders, or I could get my brother's case notes back."

"Did you find them?" I asked.

"I had them in my hands until this bloke attacked me out of nowhere." Gerrin tilted his head toward Valen, as though the larger man didn't launch daggers from his glare. "I don't know where they went after the fight."

"I wouldn't call that a fight," Valen's voice held a soft snicker.

I rolled my eyes. "Can you show us where you had them?"

Gerrin stood and retreated toward the broken window. "Can you bring the candle?"

I scooped up the candlestand and joined the man. He hunched over, peering beneath gaps at the bottom of the cupboards.

"Here they are." Gerrin kneeled and thrust his hand into the narrow opening. A moment later, he pulled them back, papers in his grip. I carefully accepted them, avoiding the areas stained with Gerrin's blood from his injured nose, and stacked them into a neat pile. It took a few more blind grasps before he seemed satisfied with the pages he'd collected.

I clutched the pile softly. The answer to who the killer was, who had threatened my livelihood, hopefully laid in these pages.

Gerrin cleared his throat. "Can I have those now?"

Of course, he wanted the case notes of his brother's death. I forced a smile and reached the pages toward him, tipping them at the last moment.

The top page slid off. Gerrin tracked it with wide eyes and reached for it.

I snatched the second sheet from the pile and swirled it behind my back. A subtle gust of air told me that either Valen or Krissa had pushed the paper toward them.

"I'm so sorry!" I said. Gerrin lifted the fallen page and returned it to the top.

"It's fine. If you're done interrogating me, I'd like to go home now. It's been a rough week for me."

"Of course." I layered plenty of influence into the word. "We're so sorry for the confusion. If your nose still hurts in the morning, come find me and I'll make you a sweet healing tonic."

Gerrin touched his nose as though he'd forgotten about the wound. "Maybe I will. Thanks, Rae."

He didn't thank the others, but sent Valen a pointed glare as he stepped back through the window he'd broken.

"Do you believe him?" Krissa asked in a low voice.

I shrugged. "I don't have a reason not to. He clearly cared about his brother. Besides, I think we got what we came for."

Valen opened his tunic, revealing the sheet of paper I'd snatched from the pile.

I caught his eye, and we shared a smile.

"Where are we taking this, Sunshine?"

"My name is *Rae*. And we're taking it to Leof's office to compare it to the sketches I left there. But first, I need to stop at the butcher's shop."

Valen raised his brows. "I think Bubbles can wait until tomorrow for dinner."

"First, Bubbles can eat whenever he wants. Second, that's not what I need."

Chapter 19

"You didn't mention it would stink so bad." Krissa sprawled across the armchair in Leof's office, one hand pinching her nose shut. I thought breaking into a marshal's office in the middle of the night would be difficult, but they hadn't even locked the doors. I supposed it made sense when half the crew worked the night shift.

The scent of hot oil blended in with the sickly smell of long-dead fish as the travel-sized burner heated a makeshift double boiler. Matilda hadn't batted an eye when I'd asked for all the fish leftovers she had. She'd stopped asking questions about my strange requests a while ago. After gathering the fish, we stopped at Brew and collected enough equipment to restock the adhesive paste I'd lost during the vandalism of my home.

Bubbles also insisted on joining us. He eyed the remaining fish parts suspiciously.

"We just wait here?" Valen tapped his foot.

"I need the adhesive paste formed before I can process this parchment. It may not even work. Impressions don't like developing on paper."

"Does the wolf know we're in his office?"

I bit my lip. "He knows everything he needs to."

I bent down to the concoction, pretending to read the temperature. The Provider would return tomorrow—today, really, since sunrise wasn't far—and I wanted Leof as far away as possible. I needed to send Krissa away soon, too. If this page didn't give us any evidence, we were all in grave danger.

The simmering fish bladders changed from a stiff dough into a softer yellow slime. I blew out the oil flame. A prepared stocking stuffed around a mug lip accepted the adhesive as I dropped it inside.

"What's that?" Krissa stepped a little closer, nose still clenched shut. Valen subtly turned toward us, keeping eye contact on the windows, but I knew he listened, too.

"I have to filter out the pieces of the bladder that didn't dissolve. Once I have a pure substance, I can reheat it into a vapor, so the fumes adhere to the prints." I gave the stocking a gentle squeeze. Hot, thick goop slipped through the fabric and collected in the mug. Perfect.

Once the mystery chunks remained in the stocking, I set it aside. With most of my belongings destroyed, I settled on the biggest simmering pot Brew had to cover the evaporating adhesive paste. The parchment and heating apparatus fit inside if I curled the page slightly.

"*Now* we wait." I sat in the remaining chair and leaned my head back. The past few days offered a severe lack of sleep. Bubbles' feet thumped as he hopped into my lap. I patted his head and his tongue flicked over his eyeballs.

"How long?" Valen asked.

"How did you end up as a mercenary for the capital?" Krissa redirected his question. Her voice sounded casual, but Valen straightened.

Silence stretched long enough that I assumed he wouldn't answer.

"There are a lot of ways to pay people for the work they do. Turns out, money isn't always the most valuable."

"That is so vague." Krissa rolled her eyes. "Are they paying you with honor or something like that?"

I risked a glance around the chair and Valen met my gaze. I wondered if his broody eyes remembered the same moment as me—both of us on the floor, looking at each other beneath a wooden bedframe.

'Tell me something real.'

"Something like that," Valen echoed.

I broke eye contact.

The mercenary put on a brilliant smile, warmer than the flames heating the adhesive. "What about you? A bit young to be a professor at a prestigious college."

Krissa's face turned a lovely shade of pink. She shrugged. "It was a surprise to my parents too, I think. But I really like numbers and order, and that took me farther than I expected."

"Can you figure out the probability of this paper having any evidence?"

She blushed harder. "It doesn't really work like that."

"It—" Valen paused.

I heard it a moment later. Faint wisps of footsteps had been meandering through the station's halls all night, but these heavy ones beat distinctly closer.

Krissa and I sprang from the chairs, Bubbles clutched in my arms. Valen moved to the side of the door, that slim blade flashing in his hand. I had no clue where he'd produced it.

The footsteps paused in front of the door. My heart pounded faster. I'd felt more helpless this week than I had in a long, long time. The knob jiggled with a slight creak, and the door parted open.

I didn't even see the mercenary move. One moment, a thin layer of torchlight seeped through the crack. The next, Valen pinned the intruder against the wall, pressed a blade to their neck, and snapped the door shut with one foot.

"Woah," Krissa whispered.

I nodded. Valen's sheer control of his body took my breath away. He didn't flinch, didn't hesitate as he moved his blade with pure precision. He knew exactly where the sword would land before he finished the motion.

I wanted to move like that. I wanted the ability to protect myself anywhere, no matter what.

I wanted to know what it felt like to have all that intensity, the power and grace of Valen's body, focused on me.

The swirl of desire, impression, and draining adrenaline clouded my mind, and it took a few moments before I realized Leof and Valen death-stared at each other over the mercenary's sword.

"Let him go," I said.

Neither moved.

"How old are you two?" I snapped and turned away. If they wanted to fight it out, I refused to watch.

I walked to the pot, set Bubbles down, and tilted the top back. Faint marks clarified on the page. A smile crept over my face. It felt good.

The three others in the room talked, but I muted them into faint murmurs. Leof had a magnifying glass on his desk, and I snatched it. The device wouldn't work as well as my own magnifier, but it did the job. I stole a blank sheet of parchment and a quill pen, too.

I lost myself in the motion of the lines of the fingerprints. The ridges flowed in a predictable curve, then bent at the last moment, or ended unexpectedly. Sometimes I followed a line that split, giving me two new flows to trace.

It resembled a twisting path of rivers, all merging to create one individual life. Only a single person claimed this particular pattern. Everyone left marks on what we touched in this world. The thought was powerful and haunting.

One ridge ended in a deepening red smudge. I pulled back from the magnifying glass to study the page. Sure enough, a distinctly bloody oval interrupted a very promising print. Gerrin must have had bloody fingers from his nose when he touched this page.

I turned it toward the light for a better angle and reset the magnifying glass. Enough detail remained before Gerrin's print to potentially identify if they matched the sketches from the glass panes and the crime scene . . .

I squinted. One faint line appeared strikingly similar. I moved the magnifying glass along the pattern, tracking the ridge, and sketching as I went.

The room had gone quiet. My scratching pen became the only sound, a symphony of determination and desperation as the sunrise counted down our last day to solve this murder. The Provider could appear whenever he wanted.

Sweat covered my palm, but I refused to let the pen slip. I had worked too hard; we had all worked too hard, to fail at the last moment.

I finished the sketch.

The three peered over my shoulder.

"What does it mean?" Krissa whispered.

"Give me the other sketches, Leof."

The wolf passed the pages. I set them side-by-side, and we all stared.

"They look . . . similar?" Krissa's words held more than a suggestion of a question.

I pushed the chair back and stood up. I lifted the bloodstained page delicately and let the word I'd seen repeatedly scrawled on the parchment, and had given mere uncaring glances, clarify in my mind.

The Erline Capital: Inquisition Investigation Case #22-00211

Caine Rosecroft Gerrin

"Gerrin is his surname." Not a question or a statement—a revelation.

"He doesn't use his forename at work," Leof replied.

I set the page back down. My hands shook. Krissa grabbed my wrist, turning me toward her. She set one palm on each of my cheeks and looked into my eyes.

"Tell us what's wrong," she demanded.

I drew a shaking breath. "The prints match. The individual who touched this paper is the same one that touched the glass at the murder scene and the windows at Siren's Sorrow."

Leof smashed his fist on the table. "Castor—that bastard. I'd like to ring his neck myself."

"No." I shook my head and pointed a shaking finger to the page. "They match that print."

The bloody print near the center of the page, where Gerrin had marked it.

"It's Gerrin," I said. "He's the murderer."

Chapter 20

Rage filled the room. Valen's was cold as the first winter's chill over my skin, but I burned inside. I wanted to see Gerrin's face when confronted with the truth.

He'd been inside my home. He pretended to care.

I clenched my hands into fists, and it felt right. Justice needed to be served here. The Provider would demand Gerrin's blood, but I had a right to it.

Valen and Leof plotted Gerrin's capture while I sat and stared straight ahead. Krissa perched beside me, still holding my hand. If they knew I planned to find Gerrin on my own, they'd do anything to stop me.

"Rae? Rae."

"Yes?" I turned to Leof, realizing too late that he'd called my name multiple times.

"Can we talk for a moment?" The marshal gestured to the corner of the room. He wanted a private conversation.

Perfect.

I squeezed Krissa's hand and followed Leof.

He lowered his voice. "You need food and sleep. Obviously, your house isn't . . . ready yet, and it's dangerous if Gerrin learns you've discovered the truth. Besides, the Provider might show up today, which is probably worse than any of that. I think you should stay with me tonight."

I grabbed his hand. The wolf stiffened and looked at the touch.

"Thank you, Leof. I mean it. But I've already talked to Krissa, and I'm going to stay with her for the rest of the day.

The Provider should come to you first, and Gerrin doesn't know where she lives. It'll be perfectly safe."

Leof frowned. "When did you ask her about that?"

The lies didn't shake me. They slipped off my lips as silken as fine honey, and just as sweet.

"Earlier today, when we worried Castor may be the culprit."

The marshal looked me over. If he expected any weakness, he found none. "Alright. I suppose Krissa's house is as safe as any. I'll check up on you later today."

I smiled. "Thanks, Leof. You're a good friend."

Valen and Krissa waited for us near the door.

"We need to leave," Valen said. "I don't want Gerrin or the Provider to confront us here."

Leof spoke to the other man. He didn't see my determination or feel those flames of revenge skirt down my skin. "We can apprehend Gerrin and wait for the Provider at Dreamer's Forest. It's far enough from Rae and Krissa's house. Hopefully, he'll leave Hallow's Promise right after the exchange."

Valen gave a stern nod. The werewolf left the office first, Krissa followed, and Valen caught my arm as I passed.

He lowered his voice. "You shouldn't stay alone today."

I wanted to feel that desire again, to savor how his words tilted with the slightest edge of concern. But the numbness stretched too deep. Gerrin had brought the Provider here, had placed me in the capital's eye again, and had ruined the only home I'd built myself.

The smile on my lips felt as cold as Valen's anger.

"I'm staying with Krissa tonight. Nobody knows where she lives. I'll be safe."

His blue eyes danced over me. I wondered if he saw my soul, the very place where ice and fire met. But he released my arm without a word.

I trailed after the others and exited the station.

Valen and Leof spoke to each other in hushed voices. Bubbles lingered near my feet, his wide expression scrutinizing me. I suspected he saw more of me than any of my friends here, and he knew exactly where my lies began.

"I need to prepare a few things," Valen said, loud enough for us all to hear. "I'll return for the search later."

He sent one more chilled gaze my way. I returned a warm smile, and the man started down the road, disappearing into the darkness.

I drew a deep breath. Only one chance to get this right. I expected my heart to pound as deceit consumed my mind, but it remained calm, steady.

I grabbed Leof's arm and lowered my voice. "I forgot the sketches in the office. Would you mind grabbing them?"

He raised his brow. "Are they necessary?"

"The Provider may ask for proof."

"Maybe," he sighed. "I'll be right back."

The station door opened and closed as the marshal stepped inside.

"Where's he going?" Krissa asked.

I looped my arm through hers, leading her toward the road. "He forgot something. Listen, it's late, and I agreed to stay with Leof tonight. You should head home." My tongue should have burned. Lightning should have struck me from the sky. Instead, Krissa tapped my hand with her fingertips and tilted her head.

"Are you sure?" she asked. "I can wait for Leof to get back."

I shook my head. Precious few moments remained before the wolf returned and my careful plan shattered.

"He's probably on his way out right now. Go ahead and get home. I'll update you when everything's done."

She yawned. "I guess I am a little tired. I'll see you tomorrow?"

"Of course."

Krissa's hand slipped from mine. Her steps padded down the cobblestones. She turned once, gave me a soft wave, and continued into the darkness.

I thrust my hand into my pocket, where I'd hidden one secret supply I'd collected from Brew earlier.

Most people thought there were two ways to obtain wolfbane: legally through healers or law enforcement, or illegally from the black market. Turns out there's a third, also illegal, way: to grow an unofficial stash amongst the plethora of other herbs under the guise of witchcraft. And my wolfsbane sprung from hallowed ground collected beneath an altar of a pagan goddess.

Power licked my skin as I rubbed the dried herbs across my arms. It wouldn't cover my scent, rather eliminate it completely, at least for a few hours. Leof probably wouldn't look for me, anyway. He'd assumed I'd left with Krissa, but the wolfsbane would make sure of it.

And by the time he learned the truth, it would be too late. I would track down Gerrin and make him pay for everything.

Somehow.

Chapter 21

The night slipped from my skin as I meandered through the gaps between trees and houses back toward Brew, Bubbles still content in my grip.

Death and darkness went hand in hand. The shadows never bothered me, not as a child in the capital, and not here in the woods. Sunshine lightened the sky as I walked, and that didn't bother me either.

What many forgot, or pretended not to notice, was that death and light also go together. Without one, the other forgoes existence. That cohesion allowed me to shift life between people. It gave me the ability to sink sentience into Brew.

And it let me become a living power as the sun rose over Spirit's Peak and offered the world a soft, morning glow.

If I found Gerrin, I'd have to use my magic.

I didn't have any other options. I couldn't wield a sword the way Valen did. My hands didn't sprout claws like Leof. No, Gerrin's life would end with a swift, punishing strike of necromantic power.

And the king, far away in his castle, would feel it and find me.

That thought broke through the numbness. My heart finally pounded in my chest, gaining speed. I froze.

If I returned to the king, he would make me use my magic in those horrible ways. I'd kill people over and over, giving him the ability to live forever.

I'd lose Krissa, Leof, Brew, and Bubbles. I'd never rebuild my house.

The anger faded. Logic clawed its way out of the depths of rage and revenge.

I didn't need to use my magic to kill Gerrin. I had an array of poisons at my fingertips, just waiting to be crafted especially for him. He didn't know I'd figured it out. Slipping him a poisoned drink would be easy enough.

Leof might arrest me, but he'd have to prove it first. I had enough options to make that almost impossible.

I resumed a slow walk. Bubbles' chest moved as he snored against me. I matched my breathing to his and let the adrenaline settle.

I wouldn't return to the capital. Not today, not ever.

Brew appeared along the edge of the tree line. I smiled at the sight. Maybe my home was ruined, but I could rebuild. Everything that truly mattered remained right here, in Hallow's Promise, and not going anywhere.

A figure stepped from behind the wagon, a torch raised in one hand. They lifted their head.

Gerrin's sharp gaze met mine.

I froze, clutching Bubbles instinctively and the warplog burped in reply.

"Gerrin," I tried to smile. He didn't know I'd solved the murder. "What are you doing here?"

He glanced at the creature in my arms and lifted his lip in a cruel smirk. "I should have known you were trouble when you saved a beast like that."

I pressed Bubbles closer against me. "What do you mean?"

Gerrin moved forward, and I retreated. He stopped, the smile growing wider. The swirls in his eyes changed from a slight twinkle to a whirlpool of darkness. An archaic power spread from his body and circled me hungrily. An ancestral remnant screamed I should run, get far, far away, but I forced my feet to remain in place. Predators enjoyed the chase.

"You're magic?" I asked, forcing a faux curiosity into my voice. My own power flared in response, and I urged it back down.

"Me? No, I never had that privilege, unfortunately. But it turns out my brother had quite a collection of enchanted items. And when he died, they became mine."

Gerrin raised the hand not clutching the torch. His flesh wriggled beneath the skin, a sort of boiling motion, rolling his arm in a sickening ocean torrent. My stomach clenched when his fingers melted and reformed into thick, wet black talons.

The kind that could pierce stone to climb into a second-level inn window.

A true, deep evil oozed from the talons. Red streaks trailed up the man's arm, sending potent power into the rest of his body.

"Oh, Gerrin," I whispered. "What did you do?"

"I unleashed *power*, Rae. Power they've been hiding from people like me."

That kind of magic came from the most evil, vile curses in existence. Gerrin's brother must have found a containment vessel, and Gerrin had broken it. The curse gave him power, sure, but demanded his soul as payment. The creeping lines would spread with each use, and once they reached his heart, his body became a vessel of servitude.

"Who are 'they,' Gerrin?"

He held one pointed claw toward me. "They, the capital, you—they're the same thing."

"You think everyone from the capital is controlling the distribution of magic?" I shook my head. "That's ridiculous. Magic is something you're born with." Or blessed with, or enchanted by, or, well, there were other ways to get it, but most of them demanded more than people were willing to give.

"Don't you see? My brother discovered the secret, and they killed him for it."

"Your brother—" I tried to remember his name, "Caine—he killed himself."

"The capital's cover up did look good. But even that asshole Castor had his doubts. He stole the case notes from me. He knew the truth, too."

I took a small step toward my wagon. "Listen. I don't know what this has to do with me, but let me make you a nice, relaxing tea and we can talk more about your brother. I'd love to learn about him."

"Stop!" Gerrin raised the torch, fumbling his taloned hand into the pocket of his breeches. He pulled out a container, shredding the linen in the process, and twisted the label toward me.

Maltha.

"Are you planning to light yourself on fire?"

His laugh sent chills up my spine. He tossed the bottle of highly flammable combustibles on the ground, carelessly. "No, this is empty, because I poured it all over your wagon. You see, one flick of this," he waved the torch, "and your livelihood goes up in flames."

My throat clenched. Brew remained still, but it must have been afraid.

"Don't." All the will, the fiery rage I'd simmered my way here, faded in a moment. Nobody knew I was here—I'd snuck away too well. They wouldn't come for me, or for Brew. "Please don't."

"I know you've figured it out, Rae. I knew the moment I saw the page missing from the case notes. You were close before, but I thought destroying your house would scare you away." He rolled his eyes. "I should have known you don't have enough sense."

"What do you want from me?"

"Want? Nothing! My brother is dead because of your kind, and you deserve to die, too."

"I didn't do anything to Caine—"

"DON'T SAY HIS NAME!" Spit flew from Gerrin's lips. His hand shook wildly. I snapped my mouth shut, worried he may ignite the maltha accidentally.

He stopped shouting, his chest heaved. "I tried to kill you, but you weren't *there*. And you're never alone. But now . . . now you are."

I swallowed. The truth hurt.

"You ran that couple out of town," I stammered, searching for anything to keep him busy, any way I could plan an escape—with Brew.

"That's what ended up happening." He studied the talon. Thick black goop rolled off one tip and smoked on the ground. "I didn't quite understand the power yet. They got lucky."

"And the Provider—you killed him."

"Of course. Nobody from that place deserves to live. Now shut up and get over here."

"No."

"Oh?" He raised the torch. Shimmering oil sparkled rainbows in the light, destruction deceptively beautiful.

"Stop, okay, I'll come."

I bent to set Bubbles down.

"No, bring the creature, too. I'll cleanse all abominations from this city. I couldn't protect my brother, but I can protect Hallow's Promise."

I clutched the warplog and stepped toward the monster waiting for me.

The talons dug into my skin as he grabbed me, and I smothered a cry. Hot blood dripped from my arm, and Gerrin smiled at the sight.

He pulled Brew's door open. Splintered fragments protruded from the frame where he'd pried the lock open, probably with those razor talons. I ground my teeth. I didn't know how, but he'd regret hurting Brew.

Gerrin thrust me inside. I stumbled to the ground and caught myself with one hand on the floor, clutching Bubbles with the other.

I drew up to my knees and turned to look at him.

"Goodbye, Rae," he said, and snapped the door shut. Sharp banging sounds echoed, and a thick nail stabbed through the frame. Brew shuttered, the floor creaking beneath me.

It took me a moment to realize Gerrin's plan.

"No!" I put Bubbles down and jumped to the door as the second nail pierced through. The door didn't budge. I banged it with both fists, putting all my weight against the opening. Not even a wiggle.

I darted to the sash. A line of nails already set in the wood.

"No, no, no. Is there any way out, Brew?"

The wagon's cupboards opened and closed.

Manic laughter sprang from outside, followed by the distinct scent of burning oil, and snaps of hungry flame.

He'd set Brew on fire, with me and Bubbles trapped inside.

Chapter 22

Brew's magic slowed the flames but couldn't stop them. Even if I used my powers to the full extent and killed Gerrin, we'd die anyway. Leof and Krissa would still be in danger once the Provider showed up, and we didn't have the murderer for him.

Heat seeped through the boards as the flames outside turned golden.

Bubbles looked at me and burped. I reached for him, but paused when red stained my fingers.

Blood, from where Gerrin's talons pierced my arm.

My necromancy couldn't save us, but maybe our potions could.

I stood up and grabbed the copper basin, lifting it from its place in the countertop.

"Brew—"

The drawer popped open before I finished asking. Rows of dried mints stared up at me. I ran my fingers along the labels.

"Spearmint?"

The wagon groaned.

"Okay, okay. Pennyroyal?"

It shuttered. I plucked the container out and upended the powder into the basin.

"Oils?"

An upper cupboard opened. The heat swelled over me, sweat beading on my forehead, dripping into my eyes.

I pulled bottles out and dropped them on the counter until the amber honeysuckle oil appeared. It joined the mint in the basin.

"Base, base, base," I chanted to myself.

The potion bases were below the basin.

"Whey or vinegar?"

Brew snapped the cupboard shut.

"That's what I thought, too." I dumped the vinegar and gave it a thick swirl. Smoke bellowed into the wagon. My eyes burned. My heart thumped harder and harder, sweat seeping through my shirt.

I released as much of my magic as I dared, blending it into the potion.

"Blood," I tried to say, but the air was gone. Only smoke and heat remained.

The basin faded from my sight. I blindly reached for it, plunging my hand into the mixture. The vinegar stung my fingers, but fumes and fire consumed all else.

I gasped, falling to my knees. The basin caught in my hand, spilling over me and Brew's floor.

My head spun. My lungs protested each tinted breath.

Brew, I thought, *Bubbles. Krissa, Leof.*

Valen.

I closed my eyes. I didn't feel the heat anymore. I couldn't taste the smoke in my mouth. A peaceful heaviness covered my body.

I sucked in a deep breath. It felt good to let go, to finally relax.

Cool wind touched my wet back.

I lifted my head. The smoke *had* faded, receded from the wagon. Flames still danced, but they no longer touched the wood panels. Brew sent another soft breeze over me, and I pushed to my knees, ignoring the shaking.

Someone outside screamed.

I forced myself up, my lungs heaving from exhaustion, and stumbled to the door. A little push shattered the burned frame, popping the door open. I spilled onto the ground.

Grass and pine needles pressed into my skin. I'd never been happier to feel them.

The scream came again.

"Help!"

I staggered up and rounded the wagon.

A swirl of demonic fire roared from a nonexistent mouth. The flames wrapped around Brew moments ago had transformed with my spell, gained sentience with my magic, and turned into—whatever this was.

"Stop!" I yelled.

The flames halted. They turned toward me, an almost humanoid figure of burning nightmares, the epitome of my rage and pain personified. It crouched down for a better look, no eyes or mouth present, but I felt its stare all the same.

I reached my hand out. "Hi."

The inferno approached, smoldering footsteps burning in the dirt. It stretched a column of fire out and brushed my hand.

Familiarity, recognition, and joy reached from the being to me.

"I see you," I whispered.

It flickered brighter.

I lowered my hand and stepped around to look at Gerrin. He hunched on the ground, burns scorching his skin.

I walked toward him, the flames following me.

Each step filled me with more power. It lit a part of my soul I never knew existed. I felt light and free, but not entirely myself. Something else lived within me, something entirely beyond this world.

"You tried to kill me," I said. My voice sounded other as that wild magic infused it. The fire-monster laughed behind me. "You hurt my wagon, you tried to hurt my friends. Tyrak Rosecroft Gerrin." I had no idea how I knew his first name. "You have defiled the Order of All, the Codes of Life and Death, and I am their harbinger. Prepare for justice."

I thrust my arms forward. My power cheered. The flames behind me lunged forward, a terrible firestorm of hell and cleansing, transformation and promise, merged into one.

Gerrin tried to plead. He tried to scream.

I never heard a thing.

The flames consumed him. They twisted and burned, eating his life, taking what he had stolen so freely from others. The cursed magic harbored in his body broke with a loud pop.

The being died. A last farewell echoed through my soul as the life I'd created returned to the world.

I staggered to my knees. A dark, smoking husk was all that remained of Gerrin.

"Well, that was unexpected."

Surprise didn't even touch me as Valen appeared at my side.

"How much did you see?" I asked.

"I got here right as the flames dripped off the wagon and turned into a roaring fire-monster."

"Sounds about right." He'd seen more than enough to understand whatever magic I held would be useful to the capital. "Are you going to tell anyone?"

He looked at me, all that glacial ice melting in his gaze. "Tell anyone what?"

"What you saw."

"I didn't see anything."

My pulse slowed. I could finally, finally take a deep breath.

"Thanks," I said.

Valen reached down. I put my fingers around his and he pulled me up.

"Were you going to rescue me?" The words blurted from my mouth.

His lips tilted in a half-smile. "I mostly wanted to see how you would rescue yourself, Sunshine."

His arms wrapped around me before I could blink. He smelled like fresh air and rich soil. I sucked in the scent until my chest wanted to explode, until my head spun for a different reason. His hand clutched the back of my head, and I realized the cool spots on his tunic were my tears soaking into the fabric.

"I thought I'd lost you," he whispered.

I shook my head. "There's always sunshine in Hallow's Promise."

He laughed, a soft vibration against my face that suddenly stopped.

"No," he groaned, talking over my shoulder. "Don't do that."

"What?" I pulled away, wiping the tears from my eyes before Valen saw them.

Bubbles had hopped beside Gerrin's body. His mouth stretched impossibly wide, wider than any part of his small body should be able to. Acid saliva dripped off the sharpened teeth and sizzled against the charred remains.

"Bubbles, don't—"

My protest came too late. The warplog slurped Gerrin's body into his mouth and closed his sharpened teeth with a click. He shifted, like trying to convince the much-too-large man to fit inside his much-too-small stomach, then belched for so long my jaw dropped.

Valen rubbed a hand over his face. "What did I just see?"

"Nothing," I said. "Nothing at all."

Chapter 23

The Provider appeared at Leof's as the sun dipped below Spirit's Peak. Valen and I waited on the stoop. We'd sent the werewolf away. Should anything unexpected happened, he had a daughter to take care of.

The Provider swished his cloak, keeping the hood up and his face shrouded in shadow.

"Do you have the culprit I have demanded?"

"Sure do." I grabbed the bowl beside me with two hands and stood up. I held it out.

The Provider waited a moment. He stretched withered hands out and accepted the offering.

"These . . . these are bone fragments," he stated flatly.

I returned to my spot on the stoop. My body ached.

"Yep." I'd swept them into a pile once Bubbles finished burping them up.

The Provider appeared skeptical despite the covering over his face. "How do I know this truly is the culprit responsible?"

I shrugged.

"I assisted in the investigation," Valen said. "It's the right person."

The Provider dropped the bowl. Bones spilled across the dirt. "Pity. I was looking forward to giving him the fullest hospitality Erline has to offer." Meaning torture, lots, and lots of painful torture.

"Is that all you require of me?" I forced my tone calm, relaxed. If the Provider asked me for anything else, I'd probably just walk into The Void and take my chances.

He must have studied me for a moment. Maybe he saw the defeat in my hunched shoulders. "No, that is all. I am pleased." He turned to leave.

"My payment?" Valen called.

The Provider paused. He didn't turn around.

"Ah, yes, of course. It will be delivered as promised."

Valen ducked his head. "Thank you."

The Provider disappeared into the shadows.

I looked at Valen. "Are you going to disappear like that, too?"

"You know I am." He winked at me, then stood up. "But maybe I'll see you again. I think there's a lot of . . . promise, in Hallow's Promise."

"You think you're funny?" I called after him.

"I know I am."

He disappeared too, leaving me alone on Leof's stoop.

Chapter 24

Two Weeks Later

"I'm still mad at you." Krissa tapped her foot on Brew's floor. I'd refinished the hardwood after the fire had damaged some parts, and I'd patched the roof, too. "You should have told me about your grand plan to hunt a murderer by yourself, then almost get killed."

"That'll be five coins." I smiled at the customer and passed along their potion. The change clinked into my box. "I told you I'm sorry a hundred times."

"That's a very small number in statistics," she answered.

"I didn't want you to stop me."

"Maybe you needed to be stopped when you were about to do something extremely stupid."

"I don't disagree. Next time I'm going to do something extremely stupid, I'll invite you."

She smiled. "And I'll say yes."

"You're supposed to stop me."

"Well, I really just want to come with you."

I laughed, the warmth from the sound soaking into my heart.

We hadn't heard from the capital since the Provider left. Leof continued business as usual, giving me time to clean and rebuild my house. I still had a few stock recipes that needed to be made, but I felt better about it all. The Hallow's Promise Library proved to have an excellent collection of books on wards, and my new ones were stronger now.

I tried to ignore the person not present, and how his absence left a slight ache in my heart.

I looked at the next customer, and crystal eyes met mine.

"Valen," I said, more of a breath than a word.

"Miss me, Sunshine?" he asked, winking.

"She did not!" Krissa yelled.

My tongue felt too large in my mouth. I fumbled to speak.

"I'll take a Brew-Licious Lavender Tea, extra sweet." He winked again. Annoyance and surprise mixed, plus a frustrating contentment deep in my chest.

I worked on heating the water, letting the lavender fragrance soothe me.

"I thought you'd left," I said.

He leaned into the window and lowered his voice enough that Krissa wouldn't hear.

"Did that make you sad?"

I leaned closer to him, letting my breath strike his cheek. "It overwhelmed me with joy."

He laughed, deep and throaty, a secret between us.

I finished his tea, acutely aware of his eyes tracking every motion. It became an almost physical touch as his gaze followed me as I added the leaves into the pot, soaked the tea with the water, and applied a thick swirl of lavender syrup around the interior of the mug. He didn't watch the drink as I poured it—he watched me.

"Here you go." I tried to keep my voice from shaking. "That's five coins."

"Will this cover it?" Valen set a sheathed short sword on my sash. He pulled the ornate silver handle from the leather holder, revealing a matching blade to the one he wielded.

Sunlight danced across the flattened side, giving me a mirror to my shocked expression.

"I can't take this."

"Sure, you can. And you should learn how to use it, too. You can't always expect a fire-monster to solve your problems."

I tenderly grabbed the hilt. It fit my hand perfectly.

"Thank you," I said, looking up, but Valen had disappeared.

I leaned out the window and caught sight of Leof approaching.

"Did you see anyone out there?" I asked when he arrived.

He looked over one shoulder. "Who?"

I shook my head. "Never mind." How did Valen keep doing that? "What can I get you, Marshal?"

"I'm actually here to offer you something." A mysterious sparkle danced in his eyes.

"What?" I asked, flatly.

"A job."

"I have a job."

"Just listen. I want you to work for me—well, for the Sherriff—officially. A title, an office, anything you need. On an as-needed basis, of course."

I pressed my lips together. Leof would keep pestering me to help investigate murders forever, especially since he saw first-hand how helpful my skills were. Getting paid added a nice incentive.

"Brew comes first," I said.

"Of course."

"What's the title?"

"I was thinking 'Crime Investigation Expert,' but I'm open to suggestions."

I leaned back into the wagon and looked at Krissa. "You hear that? 'Expert,' he said."

She rolled her eyes. "Expert Idiot."

"Hey!"

Leof crossed his arms, but he saw right through me. "So, you'll take it?"

"I'll take it," I smiled.

***

WANT MORE?
Free BONUS chapter for newsletter subscribers only!
Scan the QR code below:

Valen searches for something...or someone. Find out more in this bonus chapter.

Want to Support the Author?

The easiest way is to leave a review on your favorite reading platform. Reviews help us get visibility in the community, and spread our books to a wider audience.

Whether or not you choose to leave a review, THANK YOU for being here and reading our books.

Acknowledgements

A huge thank you to my editor, Nicole at The Assist, LLC. Thank you for encouraging me through the editing process and helping this book be everything it can. I also hope to have Bubbles merch some day. It's the dream!

Thank you to GetCovers for their fantastic job taking the terrible mock-ups I sent and turning them into art. Authors appreciate you so, so much for your reasonably and timely responses.

I'd like to particularly thank my husband. He sticks beside me through every wild dream, no matter how crazy they might be (and not just because he has to). Thank you, Babe.

Thank you to the rest of my family. New adventures start daily, and I'm always looking forward to the next one.

And finally, THANK YOU to all my readers. I love, love, love writing stories that explore other worlds, easy the hardship in this one, and give us a few moments of escape. Thank you for making that possible.

About the Author

A.N. Payton is a fantasy romance author, true-crime obsessee, and a very low-skilled seamstress. She writes at the intersection of fantasy and science, with a dash (or overflowing scoop) of romance. Her books are concocted with the perfect proportions of strong female characters, sexy men who may or may not end up shirtless, and plenty of sarcastic banter.

A.N. Payton spends her days at a top-secret job (if she told you, she'd have to kill you), which proves real life is more wild than fiction. At night she escapes by writing new worlds and problems for someone else to solve - probably with a sword.

She lives in the pacific northwest with a husband she loves (depending on the day), two kids she loves (most of the time), and a dog she loves (all the time).

Other Works by A.N. Payton

Princess Sal's magic bought her people peace and security, but she'll never be safe with the vampire king in her castle.

Centuries of war come to a bitter end when Princess Sal's parents steal half the witch army and disappear. Sal is forced to surrender to the vampire king, Kadence, and bind her magic as part of their agreement. She will give anything to protect her people – anything except her heart.

When Kadence conquers the witch kingdom, he doesn't expect their princess to be as delicious as wild honey. He can't decide if he'd rather kiss or kill Sal, and his desire for her battles against his hatred of witches. Despite their attraction, Kadence can't forget their war-torn history. He must decide if he can overcome his past to make way for a new future – one that might include Sal.

But when scouts locate Sal's parents and discover they're marching a demon army toward the kingdom, Sal and Kadence must unite their people for a final battle. If they don't, bloodthirsty demons will consume everyone they vowed to protect. Can they work together to save their people, or will hellfire destroy them all?